Lost Locks & Tales

By Janet Bailey

Contents

LIFE'S LOST LOCKS

CHAPTER ONE

BEEP, BEEP, BEEP, WENT the little monitor, she was still breathing at least, if it hadn't been for that man she believed his name was Mick, but she was unconscious. She thought she heard someone talking to her, but she was possibly mis-taken, she thought she was drugged? She couldn't open her eyes properly because they were all bleary. She didn't know where she was, but she fell back to sleep for now.

Mick thought while he lay am I alive? Did save I her? What was she called again? Annie, no, Alison, no hang on, why can I not remember? ooh wait, think. I think it's Autumn, like the breeze, fresh but awakening, one shy but strong lady. "Ouch, my head hurts a bit, and where the hell am I? In fact, where is she?" He Felt his head to see if there was a bump at the back of his head, but he was quite dazed. At this point, he heard some scuffling noises, his eyes were darting back and forth. What were the scuffling noises? Maybe mice: As he attempted to open his bleary eyes he tried to look around. He didn't even recognize his surroundings. He felt so tired he couldn't visualize properly. His eyes were almost closed. He rubbed his eyes again. His mind was spinning with thoughts, but for now, he needed to close his eyes for a moment while his brain and Adeline kicked in and didn't go into overload.

Down town, in a little part of the country, although, busy with shops and public houses and cafes, charity shops, a post office, and a cemetery, with wrought iron fences, a long driveway, and carved monuments, some of the headstones, some of the monuments are starting to lean a bit. It doesn't help to look at the mould on them. There are leaves, twigs and patchy grass slightly overgrown, same with large old church, however surrounded by trees, an old bench outside was in a sorry state, but inside the church, it was filled with drying flowers. On this day the sun had shone brightly through the window, and warmed a villager up from the slight chill, but whilst the villager was praying for forgiveness, the smell of decay at the back of the church made him leave. It could be the smell of the candles that needed replacing, but he wasn't sure.

Beyond that, there is a lovely duck pond and cottages between the town and the village, but the bus the bus only runs twice a day on the walk or bus route. Once you got into town it was near the train station and they ran pretty frequently, so it was better for those working as parking in the bigger cities was horrendous.

Walking Down further, into the main town but out of sight on the old cobbled back road which is hidden by trees, some that old are starting to split a bit. People only venture so far because there's a sign which says private road, so you only find out about the rustic cottages if you wander too far. They did find out, though accidentally by snooping, well to Mrs. B and her dog, went snooping on Mrs.

B's dog walk. She found out that one fatal day when she bumped into digger, she was a bit miffed because he had a spade in his hand. However, nothing unusual about that: he seemed friendly enough to tell her about the cottages when she asked, but what was surprising was the way he talked to her was opposite of what she had expected, he was actually nice. But he only wants a few regular people who know about the properties, to understand what goes on in there, nobody else really, but didn't say that to her.

He told her. only a few select people, mainly friends you could say, can stop there.

It was only for the exception of his little advert once a month, still it must have been coded advertisement, because it never made sense to the town or village people if they stumbled across it. Still, l really it may be people out of the village who would see the advertisement because it wasn't read by many people, but he sort of grimaced at her with his one black tooth. He did have other teeth but she wasn't looking at them, and she couldn't help but stare at him. Though he had wispy hair, and brown eyes that seemed to stare at you, but with a slight twinkle, but she did notice the big bunch of keys: one seemed to be marked with red something, maybe a dyed of some sort, they were attached to his muddy trousers, same with his spade and looked like fresh mud, not dried up that much. But she couldn't be sure she felt stupid staring at the spade, that looked a bit bent, and keys that was a bit dull except for one shiny one, it must be a new key she thought. He did pull her up for it and asked, what was she looking at and that's when she coughed a sly cough with the dog barking at this point and then they left.

Mrs. B told a couple of people about digger, about the cottages not about her findings. She may investigate more, she thought, but wanted to keep that between her and her trusty dog named Brave, because he was always brave, well most of the time she thought. Her dog had been a lovely dog that she had rescued from the rescue center down the road, a lovely clean place well-kept. She told only a couple of other Nosy parkers, one cottage, was used for a long-term, let only when the man that owns it decided he is going to rent it out. He was named digger, because people have seen him, in the distance, but Mrs. B thought it was, so they named him digger. One day she may go their pretense that she wanted to ask his name. Maybe she could take him some home-made cookies, and she wouldn't fear him. She wondered if she knew him. She admitted to the dog, she had felt nervous that first meeting with Digger. Based on the information provided. She mentioned that there are four cottages scattered in an odd manner. Out of these cottages, one of them is available for long-term holiday rentals, as she had previously mentioned. Still, it's a hidden cottage, along with the with the other three, which you cannot see from the road. It is no ordinary place excellent facilities. Two are used for short-term lets, and one has pretty curtains up, but sometimes newspaper goes up in the middle of the window, but that must be his cottage.

And yet hardly anyone knows, about this place, only a select few from the village even though villagers gossip, they don't say much about him, only that he is strange.

One wondered if he went to the same school, but wondered what his real name was they don't go down the cobbled road much because the owner is a recluse, he looks a bit shady. They wondered why he had let himself go, although they know is he must be a loner. People do take their dogs for a walk nearby but never down the private path. The villagers maintain absolute secrecy regarding the matter, however by chance one villager stumbled upon an advertisement in a monthly newspaper accessible only to those with inside knowledge of its location.

While a select few individuals know this information, the group has steadily expanded over time. Presently, they converge cottages for a singular, undisclosed purpose.

This sequence of events transpired when an individual discovered a hidden workshop while journeying down an unfamiliar road.

Digger has to make money, although must be rich people think, and so with this group and experts in the facts about mysteries and treasure, they go there with specific intentions. They go there as a meeting point, plus, years ago a select group only a handful of kids and a few adults knew of some special keys given to them by a teacher.

Now the kids are adults, yet if they go to the cottage, they tell people it is for kids/adults who just want a quiet retreat for a holiday.

Back to where the newspaper is printed is down at the workshop. The workshop gets a percentage for advertising in this special paper, but they cannot let anyone else into the select group. They don't do much now but come to discuss what may lay ahead. Was it true about some treasure? It's a mystery. The group is getting too big to share any such treasure, but nobody as yet not even kids.

Only a select few children got told and a couple of trusty friends, to opened special boxes with special on a special day in ten years when they were first buried. To their surprise, each child got a key but only six boxes were hidden, and everyone kept a pact. They knew it could be just junk, but at the time, they learned their teacher well was a bit of a loose cannon, but he had started the ball rolling, saying in ten years open these. The families got told to hide the box as a game and yet nobody was told where to go exactly, so they needed to find the map in a book, maybe they need to find the teacher. Good old Mr.

McKenzie. They need the map, very soon.

Digger comes into the village They're keep thinking they should see if he needs anything but there a bit scared of him, and yet nobody reports back what the short/long term lets what they are used for. They simply don't know.

Frank went by the workshop by accident because he wasn't concentrating, thinking about other stuff, landed by the seminar he seems to know how to get there, now at different times, which is a bit odd as he landed there by chance. But he has a brilliant memory for an old geezer.

The workshop, is made up of a woodshed, outback there is a wooden shed, someplace where they make tools, and in the back they do this little bit of printing work. Another room is where the toilet and sink is and a tiny shower room which was a pleasant surprise for a couple of part time workers. It looks quite posh, but it always smells lovely because the owner's wife Sally keeps it lovely.

There is one tinier room to have a coffee break in, but enough room for two comfy chairs a kettle, tiny table top fridge and microwave thanks to the owner's wife again.

A cupboard for cups and a stationery cupboard too, and one large walk-in room where the printer and office supplies and a table and chair and a phone is kept, with a little window to see out of all thought out very well considering room size. This paper is, about news that's a bit out there. Hence the reporters have to do a lot of snooping, and questioning, for their paper, yet information always lands their way, intentionally or not, just recently.

Digger, who owns the cottages comes into the village to buy odd bits just smiles buys bits and leaves. He doesn't smell or anything, and doesn't really speak. They keep thinking they should say something, but are still a bit scared of him.

Even though a couple people think they recognize him.

The sweet little couple, Jenny and Max lived in one of the cottages on the way to town Max works at the local police station, he is nearly ready for retirement, and his mate Ron and girlfriend Charley, she works at the local police department, in the laboratory collecting evidence from scenes of a crime in the forensics department. All these friends were having food and drinks together at Max and Jenny's as they only lived in the next street and discussed a missing peoples report, but thought they could discuss it another time during work time. As for tonight, the menu was a full chicken dinner with everything on, Jenny's specialty roast potatoes so fluffy on the inside, and crisp on the outside. Strawberries and cream and chocolate sauce for after tea. They had drinks, music, and plenty of laughter from within the walls. They did have a Jacuzzi in the garden that they may go in another day, but Max has a large shed at the bottom of the garden, and Jenny always makes jokes about dead bodies being there as it is always locked. Well they did laugh, Jenny also admitted she didn't like the basement either because it's scary: that set Charley off laughing, that set everyone else off laughing, but then Jenny got up and said "You go down there, and you will see what I mean." "Ron said "I'm sure it's not that Bad."

This particular day she announced in the next coming months she wanted to have a clairvoyant night. They all laughed that when she stormed off in the kitchen and banged about a bit opening and shutting cupboards, she would broach the idea again in a few weeks give, their time to stop laughing. She huffed a bit and then went into the room all smiles. It was getting late and they turned the music down a bit, and Ron and Charley had another drink with Max, still Jenny had a decaffeinated coffee and a few biscuits and said she was taking herself off to bed in a few minutes, but really she wanted to ask questions on her pendulum then read a fascinating crime book about facts.

The others drank for a little while longer, but a little loud.

They had to keep shushing each other up, until a car alarm went off, and that was a queue for time to go before having a look to see who set off the car alarm at this time of night, maybe a cat, it looked like someone scurrying off in the dark, like someone's shadow, but they couldn't tell properly, as the drink was flowing so well, they dismissed it.

In the alleyway there were a couple of cats, meowing. But Mrs. B even though she was a bit of a Nosie parker, loved animals and had bought a little shelter for stray cats even though her dog didn't like it much. But She didn't' really make that much of fuss about cats. He was fairly placid most of the time. However, she did have a secret word to tell her dog to attack if needed. Her x military son taught her, and the dog, what to do and what she needs to do to protect them if they should need it and her son eventually intends to get his own place. Her son nicked name was kick ass, a name given to him in the forces; his real name was Kev for short. He lives with her as he is adjusting to civilian life, and just got a part-time job starting tomorrow at a warehouse, well that's what he told his mum. Although, not really a warehouse, Frank told him about the little printing place come tool, making place workshop, and asked if they needed any-one. They said they could only pay for someone two days a week. They first thought it was for him first until he said about Kev, Mrs. B's son.

But if he wanted a job too they couldn't pay much as they would have enough people. Still if he wanted to help with investigation, they would pay commission for the stories he originally was a reporter, and he had mentioned it in passing as he was interested in their printing room. How amazing, what a gem of a place he thought. Why not I am nearly retired the extra money will be welcomed and handy, and as for Kev it gets him from Mr' B feet, until he gets used to things, then onto a full time job, maybe, or even stay here.

Down on the motorway, there was evidence of some sort of crash. The remnants were still at the side of the road.

The road had been blocked off a few days ago. Although the police had been at the scene earlier that day, the policeman named Ron just happen to be passing late at night. He hadn't seen the accident entirely but the next day when he passed again, he saw some bits of the car, and knew about a car in the compound. He wondered if it was from a car he thought he knew, and wanted to do a bit of digging. That type of car could have been anyone's, except for the little window sticker, which says powered by fairy dust.

Mind you he had thought it was from the car, that he had heard about the day before, he wasn't sure if he knew the person as he recognized the car, they had moved the car to the compound. Although the number plate had rung a bell somewhere in his mind he thought he knew the person who owned the car but not the number plate, in fact he hadn't seen the lady in question for some time, but maybe it wasn't hers he wondered, He thinks he had met her one time briefly through her mother. She had mentioned that her daughter doesn't like driving on the motorways, only the back roads, so for this car to be on the motorway was a bit strange, but he was good friends with her mother. he didn't know they were connected until recently when he saw Autumns mother having a coffee and he joined her, in the quaint little coffee shop. Ah that was a good day for him. They had given subtle glances to each other and smiled, as they both liked each other secretly. He will have to have a really good think, he knows it will come to mind sometime soon and he will try to find out. But yet, the number plate didn't need add up to whom he thought the car belonged, so now he was even more miffed why the people or person from the crash scene had left; there wasn't much evidence of a struggle only the woman's scarf, which had little fairy's on, He thought and thought I was talking to that lovely woman the other day he told his partner called Adam about Autumn, oh do you mean the one with auburn hair and big brown eyes and big lashes, Autumn, yes?" and began to tell him he had seen this woman in a café.. He had asked her name because she had dropped her coffee on his shoe in the cafe and offered to buy her another, but she insisted on buying him one too.

Seen it was her fault and she wasn't looking where she was going, he blushed because he fancied her something rotten. In his head he was smiling Adam and Autumn, until Ron said "Come on police work to be done," and saw the funny expression on Adams face, and yet it was the same cafe where he had coffee with Autumns mum, so he just smiled and just nodded his head. So, back at the station, another report had come through about a missing person, a male this time a person called Mick, "so, that is two people recently," Adam said to Ron, "hum, yes there seems to be a lot of missing people, at the moment, Let's put it to the team, although not convinced about that accident and the car, forensics got the evidence of that accident a few days ago". The number plate looked like it had been changed, and yet

Ron thought he knew the car even with its different number plate. That's what he told Adam.

Chapter Two

S CRAP, SCRAP, SCRAP. AT the workshop, Kev was scraping the tools making sure they were sharp, until Frank walked in and said hiya kick-ass. That's when the other worker laughed so loud that the secretary, well owner's wife Sally, was in charge of keeping the place running more smoothly than the owner, well she had heard from the other room, and asked "what on earth, was going on?" Frank just said.

"oh it's a military thing." The other worker said "kick ass; you have to be joking," that's when Frank just smiled and put his finger to his nose, and pointed Kev looked and smiled, leaned forward on the table and nodded like some sort of code whilst his co-worker just shrugged.

Ah, yes the very friendly retired new reporter Frank, going about his business, well, semi-retired now, who would have thought working for the commission was so, much fun?

The stuff this little work shop does is unbelievable. The printer room for the paper gets information, but they don't know who has been leaving little messages about recent events. The report investigates themselves, but to be truthful, they don't know who leaves the notes pinned to the door at night, ready to be found the next day. As for the reporters, they don't know how the information lands at their feet, there little team are pretty on the ball, but they do find out information themselves. Still, because its recently happened, especially about two missing people from a crash, that is very recent. They also receive other snippets of information, but cannot be published until full details are available. It's like someone wants to confess to something, but this is the only way they can tell people, without being seen. Maybe they could get CCTV cameras, although they don't want to go to that expense again as the cameras disappeared once before. Whoever gives them clues they are very good at their job, the person or persons never wants paying all the person or persons asks in return, is he/she leaves notes to ask for there a few demands.

It started with for food and drink, but as the stakes rose he/

she asked for camping equipment. Frank wondered along with others, if it was for a homeless couple, as two-pop up tents were mentioned, two sleeping rolls, and other equipment, so they have left food and drink. But because information is new and if it is not resolved soon, they left notes for them to say they are happy to buy equipment, but they can they come in for a chat? If they find out more, they will leave a pop-up tent for two people etc. So they will be happy each week to purchase second hand stuff leave it outside the workshop and every other day or sometimes a bit longer, if more information of news for their paper, so it's well worth the person or persons demands, they only have one reporter now as the other is on long term sick, hence where Frank comes into play, and has come to the workshop to meet with the other reporter today, to see if he is returning to work but he will be returning to work next week and help him, whom they will bounce off ideas and theories with, both will only be part time, as they don't know how the owner keeps a float, but he always has money for what they need and they do get paid, the other reporter gets paid commission too, but their job had been made easier investigating things themselves because the clues are there, technically the owner would sooner just pay the so-called homeless person or persons but never seen them, one day he may do a stake out himself and see, if he can catch him/her at this point he doesn't now, who he/she is but definitely wants to chat, the owner did leave a note so that they can even meet at night if they wish, This week hopefully.

Back to the dwelling, where the muddy prints are in the room where Autumn was, it was clear that someone had been in. she is fully awake from her slumber. She experienced overwhelming terror, realizing she was not bound or restrained in any way. Her disheveled hair added to her distressed appearance. As she touched her clothing, she realized with unease that she was not wearing her original attire. The question arose: Where were her clothes? She got off the bed very shakily and went to the door. She was tugging at the door handle, and collapsed to the floor with exhaustion, trying to open the door. She tried to scream, but nothing, came out of her mouth. She was too dry and put her hand to her throat. She needed to find out where she was. She looked up to see a vent; if she could scream towards that, maybe the voice could be carried, but at the moment, she needed a toilet, a drink, and her clothes, and find out where the hell she was, and what happened. There were blank walls all clinical walls, and then she noticed what seemed to be a door. She staggered over to the door; inside it was a small bathroom, and that where she found a cupboard with all neat, tidy and fresh-smelling clothes.

There was a water bottle and a note with tablets that would make you feel better; she didn't even touch them. She did wonder if she was in hospital or if was she dead.

Further down the corridor, which had very, very tiny windows that you could hardly see out of, outside that door which led to another room fairly similar room to Autumn, was Mick fully conscious. But he had been trying to cleverly unpick the door with a sort of rusty nail he had in his concealed pocket from work he had done days ago. He must have washed the trousers with the screw in them, and smiled. When he forgot to chuck the tiny screw away. He attempted to unlock, the lock to no avail, but he thought it would be a bit longer before he would have it open. But he thought he heard scuffling noises again, only the noises sounded like the noises sounded like footsteps, but could he attack whoever had got him hostage, although he hadn't been tied up either?

That's when the door opened, with a creek sound. He was ready to pounce on whoever it was until he saw that the person was his mate, the old Doctor. "What the hell am I doing here, and what the hell happed?" "oh, mate, you and another woman, well, you had an accident, and I am sorry, but we need to keep you, here." "what?" and that's when a woman walked in. "Don't worry, its temporary; let's just say it wasn't meant to be you two," "what, let us go then?" "well, yes, you're going to help us." "What do you mean? Help you?" "Can we get Autumn?" "yes, we will, but first, we need you to agree," "Agree to what?"

"Agree to track down, the person responsible for, well, do you remember when we were kids?" The doctor said,

"well, you took my treasure." "Can you explain, what treasure?" Mick said "or I am leaving." Or no, the doctor pushed Mick to the floor, and there was a tussle. He said you either sit and listen. And he said, "we will be back with food, and you help." Through the back of the door and I will explain later," they said.

They then went to see Autumn, and when they explained it to her, she was very furious, "I was on my way to a party surprise, party I think, but I kind of guessed, I kind of asked for it, wait I got bundled off, I thought it was part of it, when that idiot kidnapped me and took me in a stolen car," Well she presumed it was stolen; it wasn't even my car the idiot," "well, maybe, but we need your help, because you two owe us." I owe you but how?" "All in good time; we will bring you food." "What! you cannot keep me, or is that idiot here? Then she locked the door. She tried the door again but sat and waited. " Don't you worry, you will see Mick again very, soon."

The Doctor told Anne that the two people who made the blunder "are lucky to be here, really, because if anyone else had of got to them they might have been killed. Anne said "if that' stupid man, oh, it was he told me his name was Mick a friend of Felix from School; the other fella my old mate, Felix, she was their old mate stupid surprise party that wasn't a surprise; we hadn't of put them in the wrong car, and gave stupid chase in the first place;" "I know we said the red car and gave stupid chase, but who knew she was having a kidnapping experience for her party; for it to be an actual knapping; they have to help, us they know where the treasure is," "yes, but they had the treasure as kids, but they passed it on. The only real people, who knows is that old recluse. But he could have easily passed on the treasure to the people we should have been chasing, so now we have to get them to help, these two to help; if not, were going to have to think what to do with them, because they will tell."" Don't forget it's no ordinary treasure it's our future. If they don't comply, we may need to kill them. Well, I didn't mean kill, I mean, well actually I'm not sure really", The Doctor said "No, there, my old friends, don't be silly." And walked off to get them lunch. "Shouting where did Felix run to he was lucky he wasn`t injured too badly; I thought I saw him hobbling in the distance before we got to him. Wait till see him again the chicken."

Ron was investigating, At the car mechanics down at West Point to see if they had any ideas about the red car seen down on Maple Avenue, not far from their place, or Autumns, for that matter. Just before the missing person news was official, they made out they didn't know anything, and yet the garage is familiar with paint jobs. They were investigated once for forging papers, and number plates but supposed to be legit now.

Alex had mentioned, that his old mate, the homeless guy Jay, who had stopped at his a few nights ago, let him stop in return for information. He knew about dodgy dealings, number plate swops for robberies and things. Ron had spoken to Autumns family, and told all they could about the accident with the car that may belong to them. They could do was wait for news, which was not taken lightly.

They were almost cursing because, although the kidnapping was supposed to be fun, it was even a bit weird.

But she had gone on about this experience so much because it happened on the television, they thought. Right, let's give her what she wanted, even though crazy, and she had always been talking about this stupid person that does it, him and his mates. They didn't know what had happened, even though time seemed to have stopped, and the Ron had told them about the wrong car, and they had seen that red car the night of the accident parked near their red car because they couldn't park outside the house. After all, too many cars in the street.

Yet Alex had bought a second-hand car from the garage at West Point, and it had all seemed to check out at the time.

Ron and Charley had been invited over to go to Max and Jenny's again, even though it was there time to host the night, as Jenny definitely was going to get her spiritual/

clairvoyant night even if it killed her. But they also asked if Alex wanted to come, even though he kind of looked at Max with interest and asked a zillion questions before he agreed, but with hesitation. Plus, he didn't have much planned tonight so agreed, even though he knows Charley she can be a bit odd, due to working in forensics for far too long because she scrutinizes everything.

Plus he did ask if The recluse could come, the recluse D as known for digger, never really goes anywhere, moreover, he did ask if the recluse could come, the recluse D known as Digger, never really goes anywhere, but he and the homeless guy are friends and were friends and were friends from school, plus over a short period, Alex had been talking to D, recently and talked with Mrs. B and Mrs. B is still going to take her cookies after the weekend, but digger never gets invited but said yes, because he was wondering around all lost, and mumbling something about missing things, séances or something and Alex said "what's wrong with you, mate, look my friend told me about having a spiritual night tonight, you can relax and maybe you can get answers, we see you about and well, "and repeated it said withheld breath, one breath in slowly and one breath out slowly "what happened, you look like you saw a ghost and he said I did," Alex said

"what that's what we do are doing for fun tonight, believe me not my idea, but my mates wife is a bit loopy like that,! well what, come on fella, tell me all about it. Let's get to Maxis house; there is no such thing as ghosts,"

D went cold and said one sentence "let me tell you, there must be two x wife's then I saw my x wife walking just walking, thought she was dead.

She went out for a walk one day never returned. she hand-ed me some weird keys, before she left, which I put away and hide so not to be reminded of her; now she's well either a ghost or alive." Alex thought he had been on the booze, but told him to come with him; maybe the spirits can give him answers or not. "Look, leave it till we get there, and we can put a report at the station tomorrow, when you're feeling better, I've seen you; in town, but never made the connection till now. Plus, I do know you we all went to the same school.

So with anticipation on both sides, they arrived with curious looks from the gang. but they were all accepted for now, explaining how they met and realized everybody was connected by the old school; even Alex had bought a drink for people to share along with others. A bit of whispering went on, and a few blank stares at Alex who had bought these strangers, as they thought who weren't a stranger after all; they weren't bothered but he did interest them. Same with Digger.

The night had bought about D. His real name actually was begging, with D. was actually called Des, but he knew people called him Digger, but he wasn't bothered.

He knew he looked odd and wondered if he should start making himself a bit tidy. considering he actually likes his homeless friend's girlfriend. Maybe she has a friend. He wandered outside for some fresh air, quickly followed by Max, who chased after him. He didn't want anyone by his shed. Which definitely got his back-up; he only wanted to see what size it was inside, so what did Max have to hide.

After the bizarre weekend of near mishaps, unsettling news, and possible strange encounters, a book flew off the shelf that made them jump, but Jenny will look at tomorrow. Firstly, she wondered how and why it flew off the shelf. It could be a silly prank from others. Second thought, it opened at the back page; they never saw any spirits, and yet fell open.

Nothing else happened, but Charley asked, what was in the shed, but Max sort of gave her a funny look.

Further into town, Mrs. B was making her cookies, yet, she was chatting away to brave her lovely dog, telling him her plans, when Kev walked in, asking if any of the cookies was for him, and nodding his head when she was talking to the herself and the dog lost interest and fell asleep.

The cookies smelled like fresh cookie smell fresh coffee, home-brewed was perfect. And she had nicely picked flowers in a vase on the table along with a bowl of rosy apples; she got everything ready, then got his lead with a reluctant dog and off to see Digger. In fact, she was intrigued, because she was actually thinking, he may look odd, but she wondered what he would be like if he had a haircut and wore smarter clothes. Beneath that grin what he is really like, why had he let himself go that much, and what was hidden in the cottages.

Digger was having a clear-out, when his x wife appeared from nowhere, and he nearly fell to the ground, grabbing the side of the door, and immediately went to the chair, he nearly couldn't get the words out to enquire what she wanted, and went into a whole spiel about why she was here, what happened, and why was she back. She wanted the keys but why? Why should he give them to her, and why did she leave? And this conversation went on for a few hours, then knock, knock on the door outside was Mrs. B

who interrupted them with her cookies, at the door, and Mrs. B was a bit upset to find someone there, was it a person who was letting one of the cottages? He said "don't worry she is leaving." His x wife left and shouted, "I will be back in a few days, for them I asked for," and left. He then told Mrs. B she could come in, He wasn't smart, but she said "your looking better with a haircut" and he smiled with that glint in his eyes. He hasn't spoken to many people over the years but actually started to shine after his visit to maxis' house, but he is still curious as to what was in the shed.

His realization came flooding back, when Mrs. B was talking, and suddenly went quiet and drifted off for a minute.

He shouted out "we are all one; we all went to the little school, and she looked and said "Des, is that really you?"

frankly talking and bravely enjoying a cookie too with them, just looked at Des as if he was meant to be there.

"The keys" he said and told her he would be in touch.

He may need her help. He needs to do something first.

"What, why, and what do you mean?" He realized this was the year, this week or next. He realized this is the year they were told to open the boxes this year, this week or next, he wasn't too sure. Ah, so that's why his x wife is back; the keys is for the box, the realization dropped on him like a ton of bricks: Who has the boxes, and what's in them?

she couldn't possibly know where they were. He thinks he knows, where some are. The possible future treasure the moment of truth. They've been leading to the truth in their meetings.

Mrs. B left but intended to go back. She was thinking and thinking, she quietly was talking to Brave and mumbled something about treasure, the pact she remembered the pact, all them years ago. She shouted at Brave "Oh god, Brave, the treasure I had forgotten-oh who had the boxes?

Wait a minute, Brave, and he looked up at her with big brown eyes. I have to remember. Why can I not remember where they are? who has the boxes?" in fact we never really knew what was in them; who would know? She just could not think for now, when she got home her mind was whirling around she couldn't even sleep that night tossing and turning all night.

Wow, what a read! Jenny thought, the back page said it all; she went to see if Max was in the shed. He was banging about earlier. She opened the shed door where was he and omg, she put her hand on her head with one hand and with the other and half covered her eyes. This is it, one of them funny looking keys; she was just about to pick it up when Max growled at her, and she inquired where he had gone, and she had her hand resting on something covered up and she asked "what was in there," and that's when he said "this week only, I have to get to the others so we can open them." She looked at him to say your mad, but she put her hand on his and told him to come inside and discuss what was wrong. She told him about the map she had found in the book, and he told her everything.

Chapter Three

The homeless man introduced himself as Jay, and the workshop owner, whom they exchanged pleasantries. I'm Bob, so you're the one and who has been leaving messages, but why? "Do you want to know why? I know a few reasons: I observed but I wanted to help you. We were friends at one point, remember? But I will tell you, I'm in Love with Sally.

But hear me out first; I met Sally and have fallen for her, but you took my girlfriend in high school" "what?" "You know you did when we had the school dance. You took her, from me." Bob was just about to speak when Felix and Anne came in as if nothing had happened to Felix except a hobble from a hurt leg. She had enquired what had happened to him, but they didn't tell or even tell the good doctor. They left him at a special location and said, "we are here for your key," "What key?" You know which one," Bob refused, no, the key is mine, and if there is some sort of treasure its mine too," You can go to hell, but we all have keys, remember, and I go back, I danced with your girl, that's all," said Jay, then out of the corner of Bobs eye was Autumn, the love of his life all them years ago. Autumn suddenly remembered, too; he may be older, but he used to hang by the school fence all them years ago; she used to hang on to his every word but dare not get too involved. She spaced out for a minute remembered him. Bob from school, her long lost sweetheart from school, well more a crush on an older boy, and too close for comfort.

She also remembered recent events that bought a kind of grin, as she remembered her recent plane ride. But in the meantime, they were all screaming at each other, when mick came in knocked Bob out sort of accidently on purpose because he had to show his authority. He thought, after his last blunder, he knew things had gone wrong, but actually thought he had been kidnapped. Still, they needed his help, as he believed Bob would try use the power of knowing how to make tools which could be used for the wrong purpose. Bob definitely didn't want to be involved in any criminal activity, so he sorts of shoved him a bit, and searched for the special key. Well, if any extras there but false information, along with the others, there was a mad scramble when all of a sudden, the doors got closed hard from the outside. They thought it had been locked, or even trapped except for Mick and Sally with the key.

"Sally said we need to open the door, we need all the keys and the map, which looked to be here but other places", so they all needed to look as they were surprised to see other people had maps.

That's when Autumn realized she had been hurt. she clung to the table, trying to hold her side; she had gotten pushed by accident, but on doing so, she banged her head by accident when the others rushed around like lunatics. Bob woke up asked if she was okay, and then that's when she remembered another time on an airplane ride. (Going back) That lovely day as it happened it was Autumn time, which makes her giggle and Grinch too because she knows where her name comes from and thought, why did my mum and dad call me that just because it was Autumn when she was born? However, she liked the name, and her friend told to her at the airport, "be careful; I thought you was happy. You don't need to meet some random stranger, it's a long way for a blind date, and do you trust your other friend and her boyfriend?" "Don't worry; its fine if he's well a looser, or an idiot. I will catch the next plane home instead of the few day break." "You, better video chat then so I catch up to speed". They waved goodbye, but her friend had her fingers crossed. She was smiling but worried for her long-standing friend from being young. They always shared everything, but this was different. She had bumped into another old friend from school not so long ago and said she was going to Amsterdam for a few days, but she would have to catch a different flight because hers was booked, and she agreed to meet her at the hotel, where she could meet her new man and his mate, like a blind date. Maybe go to her boyfriend home after.

In the meantime, she could hear voices, which sounded familiar to Bob, but she wanted to remember her journey on the plane, so stayed in her consciousness, with her eyes shut for a few minutes. I remember her asking the airhostess and the guy next to her if she wanted a drink.

Her mind had wandered off, wondering what her blind date would be like. She then realized what was asked she said she would like a cup of tea, and the man next to her had offered to pay and asked if she wanted a glass of wine. She refused politely and said maybe later. She realized what she said, and then he said "I may just take you up on that." She blushed; she met his eyes, and he introduced himself as Mick." He then went to have a bit of a way about him-in fact, quite cute-and said her name was "Autumn." He thought how lovely she was and complemented her on her name. They didn't realize the time, she climbed over him to get to the toilet, but as she was a bit clumsy fell onto his lap, even though he was trying to stand up, and fell with her in his lap, even though he was trying to stand up, and that's when she blushed again, and franticly got up. He said "I will get you that drink in Amsterdam if you Tell me your hotel." She dashed to the toilet, wondering what had just happened. Was he trying to flirt with her? If so, he was doing a good job, and then she woke up with the others.

Bob got her hand to help her up and out of there; as they got the door they thought locked was open, she said "Where's that idiot Mick." She mumbled to herself, he couldn't even he couldn't even get a surprise right. she thought, "That idiot from the plane I wish hadn't shared my kidnapping idea with him. What was I thinking?" It's not like it would be fun.

He and his stupid friend, it was supposed to turn out nice, now look, she thought we have another issue, now look at us at us all scrambling to get the treasure, if it a treasure, they all met outside even Sally and Mick were waiting for them, with everyone fuming, that's when they realized that everyone was interlinked in some way. They started chatting now about the next step forward. Calmed down, they realized they needed another map or indication, but realized it was to another location. This might have been the first, and a couple of others from Mr. McKenzie's class may know where the so-called treasure, of their future is.

(Kev had fallen asleep in the toilet of the workshop. This is his dream from when he was in the Military and earlier) Ah, his sweet neighbour Jenny at the time, and his old pal Max, he remembered them waving him off the military at just seventeen along with Charley at the time. They weren't in for long but served. The four years Kev came out because his kick-ass reputation wasn't good, and he needed to calm down. He wasn't bad; he became a prankster after been pranked just once. The one day he was thinking about was when he pranked someone by putting shaving foam in someone bed, and went wrong for him because he picked a prank with wrong person who had a few good friends. He was on day shift but this particular time he went out with his buddies; on a night out and they were all drunk, they put him outside and decided to well undress him and leave him with not much on and waited to see who would find him there and hide his clothes. The next day he woke up with a scrabble, trying to locate one sock one shirt until he got them but was late for roll call.

So, hence where kick-ass comes in because one he was a good fighter, but two he got even with six men in his barracks as he always managed to get his own back by telling them horror tales that was made up. Laughable, really, but he did smirk then wake up. In fact, he has to see Max about the first box and keys and see where the map is. He went outside to find people who had gathered, and wondered what was happening. He was just about to ask when people went off in all directions; he now needs to get to Maxis' house or Charley's even to get the key, as ten years is almost up. Plus, he needs to go to the school, or find out where Mr. McKenzie lived, so he went to see if he can look him up on his computer at home.

Adam was talking to Autumns mum, in the usual café. To his panic he realized she was upset, because she hadn't heard from Autumn, and she was panicking and he wasn't much good at calming her down, but was trying his best.

Ron walked in wondering what was going on.

Back at the station, Charley had been in the lab, given some sort of evidence of an unsolved crime, and chatter about the person who bought it, Mr. McKenzie, the school teacher. He said he was an x policeman. But the police station hadn't heard of him, but he did checkout as a teacher with all the correct paperwork. Mr. McKenzie, was a very astute man, and very clever, in fact probably too clever for his own good, but he never seem to age that much, maybe by a few years, but considering he has been at the school ten years now, its seems a bit odd, the kids love him, over the years but as time has gone, other teachers has suspected he has a double life, because he seems too good with the students, he is always pleasant, but looks like he is worried all the time like some sort of mystery, they have asked him to go on a nights out ,he rarely says yes, he did on the last Christmas party as follows, they was all dressed up but although he did go on this night, they were glad but surprised, and they liked him ,they couldn't get much sense on what he did in his spare time, but he did have a way of interrogating them without them knowing, except one very clever teacher she was only young, but she was fascinated with him absolutely fascinated.

She went out of her way to walk him home, not the other way around; she didn't live far from him, but he was a little drunk, and she had to know what his secret was, he was very debonair, mild-mannered and yet still this air of mystery. The young lady, nick-named Flower, always wears flowers in her hair because she is little, cute flower.

She has short, thick hair, a button nose, and nice, bright eyes. She intends to finding out what Mr. McKenzie what he does on his days off. He is older than her, so she is a bit guarded, but he is so interesting when she speaks to him in his classroom, without earshot of the others, she wants to be mates with him. but Still, she didn't know if he would accept she would that, but on the way home, she thought she would see if he wanted to go to the historical museum next week or even the science one. She wants to call him by his proper name but has, yet to ask.

Back at the café when Ron told Adam about his note where to meet with his key, but he has to try remember where it could be all these years ago, without revealing too much until he was sure he could trust Adam. However, he said that he had lost a key and had to find it. Over the next day, people who had lost their keys had to try work out where they had lost or had they given them away, thinking it was all nonsense. But each individual ended up mysteriously with notes to various locations, or maps.

Ron saw Autumn's mum again, this time walking, past. He is too fond of her, and the same is true for her, she knows he is married. She is married as well, but little fantasies come into their heads. He spoke to her again and looked very concerned. Adam, caught some of the conversation but not all of them, just about in earshot, and he was going to question Ron later, to find out what the mutterings were about a box and a note, again with secrets. Now he was involved in one way or another because Autumns mum looked on and looked in Adams direction. This was something big going on. This time, he is definitely going to ask more questions.

Down by the cottages, Mrs. B was snooping at Diggers place when she was tried to find him. She realized one of the doors to the cottage was open. She cautiously opened the door, peered through it with a slight squeak, and told Brave to be quiet. He started to barge in and sniff around. She called him back, "shush, Brave, stop that. What are you sniffing at?" Brave pocked his head under a newspaper. The newspaper was scrunched up, but she opened it up, she just scanned the page and noticed an advertisement about this cottage, one of them, but it was a bit odd advertisement like a rental. Still she reread it, and then once more, and then she saw it, the paper, had stacked strips of paper and a magazine, which had glue on and cardboard stuck to the magazine, like a separate compartment. She was going to rip it open but thought she had better not. A picture of an older lady, and gentleman, maybe his parents, was on the wall, but she turned to look through the window. In the distance, she thought she saw Digger, and she felt very vulnerable and anxious. She told brave, to be brave this time. Come on, "let's see what he's up to," he didn't seem so brave this time. "I have to know," she said and carefully backed out of the door, and she felt bit like a spy. She kept her phone silent, but texted her son to meet at the cottage.

This was unusual for her because Mrs. B is always brave; not so much this time, but with bated breath, she went for a closer look.

When she finally got up to him, she acted so casually until she nearly fell into a hole. "What the hell are you doing here," she hadn't heard him speak like that before. A bit sharp, she stuttered at first. That's when, she looked beyond the hole, that was his x wife, and she shook, put her hands to her mouth, and no scream would come out.

He said "it's not what it looks like." "you killed her". "No, look, she not dead; that when her phone texted, but lucky it was on silent, she thought. Although it did vibrate in her pocket, and she panicked for a second, she knew she couldn't answer it. she backed off and tripped. He said,

"I'm getting help. It was an accident, and that's when she ran towards the cottage. That's when she remembered what her son had taught her about telling Brave the attack words, but Digger shouted "Calm down," and he wanted to explain. He ran in the other direction, due to Brave trying to catch him, and shouted "let me explain", it's an accident; she was trying to get the keys." But she didn't hear straight away but she thought twice, that's when she called Brave off but was reluctant to talk just yet, she needed to know his secret. What goes on in the cottage and had he called for an ambulance?"

Chapter Four

THE STRANGE COINCIDENCE, WAS these notes were turning up like a mystery. The next note to be found was as follows. They found out that the car in the accident had a key and a note in it, the note was made with strips of paper, not a ransom note, but it was like someone couldn't write properly or something, and had to use newspaper. Still, there was a key and on the note a meeting place, which was very odd. Charley and her colleague had given evidence to Adam, who then told Ron, and eventually, between them and Max and Jenny confessed about the map in that book; it had loads of locations marked off, which means that other people had keys and notes to locations, starting with the church, due to work commitments nobody except Max could go today, but promised to meet with the others later. But Jenny was finishing early, and she has asked Charley to come with her to her house; she was going to venture into the basement and needed support. Whilst her husband is out. She was desperate to know what was down in the basement. There, she had always been scared because her parents let her stay up late when she was younger, and she watched a horror film involved a basement and a killing. It left her scared, and nervous, fearing that something might jump out at her. However, with her pal's support, she was determined to face her fears and venture downstairs.

Later that day, she waited for the coast to be clear in her house. Charley and Jenny accompanied her as they descended cautiously, step by step. As she reached for the light switch, the whole place illuminated, revealing the well-worn steps and creaky boards, some of which seemed unsafe. When they finally got the bottom step and didn't know what they had come to, what was this really her basement?

There were a few cobwebs on the low beams and a sofa bed, or sofa that she hadn't seen before, that was facing away from the steps, and beyond that was a little fireplace, and at the side, a little window may be enough for a small person to get through. They could see an old-fashioned type chair with wooden handles, facing away from the steps. As they entered the basement, they went to the table, and at the side of the table was a basket full of old newspaper cuttings, scissors, and a map a big map of locations dotted around different parts of the town and beyond. That's when Mr. McKenzie and the homeless guy jay was there. Jenny said "What the hell are you two doing in my house? Are you in cahoots with my husband?"

the sound from behind was "Darling", all sarcastic, "you shouldn't be down here," they turned round in shock,

"what the hell is going on" Max said, "well dear," she hadn't heard that tone before, "you have stumbled across Mr. McKenzie's great plan, and we will find the killer," "You better explain," she said, and he said "Sit down. Sit down all of you."

"Here is an update, let's start with the killer thing. You see my dear, a little boy was accidentally killed when we were all younger, Well, one boy drowned; the body found recently, but there was a mysterious accident occurred.

Over a boy, one of our friends had gone missing, never to be found. How and why was there was one last missing one? That's where Mr. McKenzie, comes in to find out the truth: somewhere, possibly in our basement, a child was kept. Truth is, I didn't have the heart to tell you, "Tell me now," "Well, let's just say I'm helping Mr. McKenzie out.

It was before we bought this house, so possibly the last owners fled, and that is why we got the property cheap, but on Des, Diggers land, he may have our box, the box of Destiney because it has too many secrets. He uses his land to keep the boxes hidden and also of treasure; that's why the child was held for ransom, but the family disappeared, so we don't know how, what or why? So, the Digger has expensive property and maintains the land, but people in the know stop there to swop treasure or for currency not legal. That's why it's all shush, shush till now."

"wow omg."." how do you know," let's say I of found out, with your dad years ago he was friends with Digger at school, and was given land to store old boxes, that may be valuable, as long as your dad let the land to Des, he could keep the property and they could bury treasure, he was involved with the kidnapping of the little boy in this basement, for money, but the couple who had this property, before we fled and one boy never to be found again?

Because your dad didn't like me much because of my bad lad image, he let me date you, and that was that, now you know the truth" She just about passed out from the news.

Mr. McKenzie has to go now to find his destiny.

Along with Jay, they went to see what may be in store.

Jenny and Charley couldn't stop crying at this point, hugging each other, but they had work to be done. They pulled themselves together, started their investigation, and called her dad before the police could arrive. He said "Thanks for the tip; She was he was shaking while she was talking, in the meantime, he had his bags packed with a passport ready for the longest holiday yet.

Digger and his x wife, he desperately need her to be alive.

To find the box with the orb to discover their destiny." but, how what?"

Sometime later, Ann and Felix were plotting as usual. They were bullies at school and still bullies now. They dealt with the garage to blackmail it so that they could do robberies in stolen cars; they had told the good doctor a lie, and they were very good friends but didn't want him involved any more than necessary. They blackmailed the garage owner because some years back, the garage owner had been losing money gambling and these two had money from robberies. For him to keep in business, and give him money to pay his debts, he had to change number plates.

Over time the garage has managed to sustain a good business and is now on top and no more gambling and all debts paid until the so-called last job with the one car that was in the crash, which made the garage owner very anxious as he deals all on the straight and narrow now.

Anne and Felix also received a note telling them where to go to collect their box, but first, they were told to confess about a stone which had blood on it from all them years ago; if not, it was their turn to be blackmailed but from whom? So, now it was a race to get to their destination to find their box of destiny, and yet the tables had turned;

the sense of urgency was imperative, and the glee of the Garage owners' delighted when they fled quickly was a relief, hoping they wouldn't go to the police. When Adam recently acquired his new car from them, they had to made sure it was a genuine second-hand car no bogus cars or number plates.

Back of the church, there was that musty smell again this time. The new vicar decided, he was going to clean this place up again and get it fit for purpose, but the smell was coming from near the candles, only to find a bag that he most certainly had not noticed at first. He couldn't understand why such a beautiful church had been left in such a sorry state. However, the last vicar left rather quickly, he was poorly, and couldn't attend to the grounds, they have new grounds people now, but there was a bag un-attended, he cautiously opened the bag, and had to hold his nose he could hardly lift the bag and called the police, someone had left a bag there, and the smell was of a dead child, which made him very ill, he was gagging all the way to the bathroom, he returned to find in the bag, the hair that remained was matted and wet, along with the bag and a nice puddle all over the floor. It caused an investigation into the lake where a school boy was identified who had been believed to have drowned years ago but never found. But since the water level had fallen in recently, someone must have discovered the body but didn't want to report it and left it in the church. Somebody must have dragged it there at night-time as not to be seen.

There was also a discovery in jay's hand, in a bag, and held it up and said to Ron, "look what I Found in maxis shed, and Charley nearly was sick, Jenny's dead dog, that had gone missing. She had been looking for it ages ago; even put up flyers to see if anyone could see it. Jenny ran upstairs in floods of tears, crying and crying she couldn't stop. "why, oh Why?" That's when the gang was here, and Max said "That flaming dog, followed me everywhere,"

"What." and she cried again, "yes I hated it." "but you loved it." I did until she bit my ankles, when I found the box in my shed. But I didn't get chance to open the box because you lot was meddling, and that the dam thing, I had borrowed Desis spade and made it, look, like it wasn't me, I confess, so sue me," Des and Ron had arrived at the house. Des had come to ask what the red markings were, on his spade, which he had borrowed the other day, why he had been such a bully at school. Everyone questioning him. Well not anymore, he's said "you know why? I'm here I take it you confessed and reckoned you didn't know me for ages. Well, guess what the tables are turned because we can know see the future. Yes, that's right, the map, we will get the box of truth. Jenny said "I'm calling the police, "Max said No, you won't because if you don't get your key, you won't get your destiny, "why did you kill my dog really?" "Look! I don't want you or your stupid dog."

That's when she lunged for him, but the others stood back and just shouted, "No he is not worth it."

Jay said "Come on, let's calm down, Des said "Look, Mrs.

B, a lovely lady came after me, then her son, but in the end we made it right. I told them the truth, about the property, belongs to me left by my grandmother, but came a snooping conclusion. You know I was blackmailed into using my land for conspiracy's and, well you know the rest, yet I rented them out, and people wanted to use them for Their own agenda, and yet you used me: the idea came from you about Anne and frank kidnapping Autumn and yet where is she? Mrs. B she worked it out now; give me my key that you found on my land. With everyone aghast saying "what?" and arguing, he then came to Jenny's to get the map, with everyone out of the basement now, to make sure he got the right spot, on his land. He needed the book when Ron said to Max you're under arrest for the murder of Desis wife," and that's when Des had to grab a chair and was shouting, and shouting then weeping, with everyone staring. "No, she not dead, I've seen her today," what?" "yes she's ok, she fell; she was fine," Ron said, "who is the body down at the old school, the boy that drowned, got found in the church too, but there is whereabouts of little boy now a man probably young man abroad What? "it's just been called in," Charley shouted and ran out the door, as she was leaving, she said "Mr. McKenzie, he knows followed by Ron and Jenny. Sirens were going off all directions, and heard from all over town. They all had agendas now, and Autumn was last seen catching a plane to Amsterdam, Adam was involved now and has contacted Autumns mum to say "Get Autumn home quick. She is not safe, the little boy the friend of hers, and he was babbling on, and on. Chaos was everywhere people running here and there following notes and maps.

Time was of the essence, everyone who had keys and lost keys had to be found quickly. It may be that rubbish or treasures will be found, but either way, here goes, from the beginning. Going back.

This is what happened: Autumn was lying on the floor trying to un wedge her hand from underneath the wardrobe; as she opened the wardrobe, she had her key in her hand and dropped it and the key had got stuck underneath the little blighter. Finally, she thought to herself, that she needed to get to the Airport, again time only very quick and cheap stay, as her friend had stayed with her boyfriend apartment, and try get a job and paper work to work, Autumn couldn't have any more time off work, after this, but she can stop with them whilst she finds the box and not in the hotel and possible date with an x vicar an older man for coffee, but she wasn't sure, with the possible help from her friend, what the box was doing there only Mr. McKenzie knew.

All she knew was last time she went on that so called blind date all she could think again was Mick the one that drives her mental but cannot stop thinking about, this time was different it was a necessary journey, she bumped into Mr.

McKenzie, purely by chance as she got in her car after freeing her hand and rubbing it in the car, before she goes anywhere she mentioned the pub again, this time as she had sat quietly nestling a drink for ages, in the pub, she needed time to think ,she never goes to the pub on her own, and this moment Mr. McKenzie walked in and he was contemplating his strategy of how to get the evidence to catch a killer from years ago, a little boy, it plagued his mind of a mystery unsolved, and the possibility of an a boy that must be a lot older now, who went missing, and possibility he is in Amsterdam, if his theory is right and Autumn is the link, this time he was going to solve it. He needs his box to uncover the killer. You wouldn't think not long since all the fuss but he needed to calm down.

When he saw Autumn he was delighted again that he caught her, before her travels she was one of his best students, but could never tell her, she has such away with her, he interrupted her thoughts asked if he could sit there as it was lucky he had seen her, and who walks in the door but flower, she took one look at him and Autumn and put two and two together, got the wrong end of the stick, and walked out almost in tears. She didn't know whether to walk in again or walk home, she didn't want to go out with him but she was jealous because that's her friend she hoped and nobody else's. She didn't even know he goes to the pub; he must be upset about something. She thought that for him to be drinking, unless this is one of his secrets, her mind was wandering all over the place.

shall I walk in the pub act all causal? Oh god, what to do?

Mr. McKenzie, actually told Autumn, asked her if she got her passport, and told her that as her friend hadn't bumped into her by accident the first time, he had to get her to Amsterdam and thought she would stay, oh because she had always said she would love to travel. Still this time was her fate. How did he know? He said it too loudly, "I have been entrusted with time, and keeper of the keys, "he put his hands over his mouth, that's when flower had walked over and started jumping up and down she had heard the full conversation, and said "I knew there was something, something big." He said, "I knew you would follow me, I was meeting you later, at the museum, but the moment I met eyes with you, although you are young, the questions you ask me, you are the one, you are part of our destiny.

She blushed and squealed with laughter, but in a good way. friends for life, oh this is Autumn, fellow student.""

Meet Flower." friends for life.

A bit later, Autumn frantically, went back home to now make sure she had her passport and clothes. She didn't even know what she had packed just a jumble of clothes quickly gathered together. So, there she was in her trusty red car, or so she thought, until she was going down her back route, she didn't know why she didn't get a taxi, but she was rushing to the airport, her steering was becoming unstable and unusual noise, and the car was slow she had to pullover at the side where it was safe. She was nearly crying when she saw the puncture, when luckily Adam and Ron, although Ron didn't look his usual chirpy self, was passing, she told Adam he was a super hero, he was the one that helped, which made him smile. He went out of his way to take her to the airport because him and Ron was on a mission anyway; he would sort her car out, if he gave him the keys and offered to take her for a coffee when she was back ,he was no mechanic and couldn't change a tire, it was there day off, and have to collect others after, she looked and put her hand over her mouth, she asked if they had been given a note, a special one, she worked it out, on the journey to the airport, she said "good luck with your Destiney", Adam looked and Ron said "oh he will be waiting for your return, good luck too." Adam then nudged Ron, and sort of nearly did it bit too hard.

Later, Mr. McKenzie had been taken to the police station for questioning. After grueling hours, he was let go but a mad dash to the school and open the cleaner's office, he needs the key and fast when the cleaner asked what he was doing there on a weekend, "same reason you are", they both tussled over the box on the floor which had the keys in. As they scrambled, the cleaner was chucking chairs about. But then Mr. McKenzie went onto the stage and carefully opened the box with the one look of the cleaner with open eyes, firstly they saw the globe to which showed what, at first they both came close, to look inside it showed a box a jewel and stone in a box the race was on. Mr. McKenzie shouted "yes, I have proof of the killer. If I get the jewel can go home at last and the cleaner looked flabbergasted, and the jewel and the cleaner said "what's in it for me they looked in the globe again; his destiny was in another box somewhere in the school.

When they find that they find his destiny, yet another note saying, where it was.

Back to now, After, everyone had dispersed from the house, they went different ways. The clay felt sticky and was saturated from the rain. Although it was starting to dry, thin bridges had formed, Jenny, was covered in mud, Max had been apologizing on the route here; he didn't mean any of it, he had said that Jenny's dad had finally said where the key was, and they followed the note, their destiny or not. She was covered even more from head to toe in the mud, and Max almost fell on top of her whilst he slipped a bit on the mud; parts of it was starting to dry. Even though a storm was brewing, when they finally came across something hard, at a tree it was on the map the third tree on the left, by the oak tree. When it started to rain some more, they needed to dig further, when a dog came running up to them, and they couldn't see what they were doing, on doing so a voice in the distance was

"what's wrong brave where are you? "Brave was barking and barking they all needed shelter, but the weather was too bad now, it was lashing it down. Mrs. B was shouting and shouting, that when another voice appeared from behind Mrs. B, and as she turned round, saw Digger with a spade in his hand, saying let me explain; please, she is not dead, you know she's not, she tried to run towards the barking and that when she fell on a landslide, with Digger running after her with shuffle in his hand.

They needed shelter and fast, but the tension was building, as everyone going in different directions Mrs. B was hurt, she was trying to hobble towards the barking, Jenny had followed them as they needed to see the globe too, in the nook of a tree buried, they had found them because they had been busy looking, their note was the same as there's about the tree that leads to the woods and there at the other side of the woods under or near a rock is a hole with a box in, they didn't want the police to find them before they found their destiny and ended up finding Mrs.

B and Des running in the wet mud and rain, Was trying to dive near rocks and Digger got confused totally and lost his way, and ended up by the water, tying to cling on to the surrounding trees. Then hurt his back trying desperately not to fall down the river bank. He yelled out in pain, that when he saw a fox in the distance hoping he wouldn't be lunch, the rip in the water was strong, he was desperately hanging on, he couldn't hand on with the wind, and so the slope down the river, made it worse. He had h a mad scramble to catch his breath, trying to use his spade as leverage and get to the side, and all he could do was lay there until the rain stopped and the wind calmed down, try find Mrs. B and get to the box. There Destiney relies on it, good or bad.

Chapter Five

Autumn and her friends thought about how lovely the caves were. They had time briefly to explore the castles ruins, once a stately residence, with its high walls and became ruins through the war, but how to get away from the tour guide? Well they had a plan. Autumn would dis-tract the guide to see if she could lure him from the cave, which was on the left behind the so-called passage and was a key, according to the note she had written. But he couldn't be easily lured away and quickly gathered everyone up. The tour guide was great, but they needed him entertained while they got the key, but how? Autumns friend came up with a solution, so through the dark tunnels they went, where people used to stay, they would try get his pass off him, they could see the so called locked door, they looked on the map it could be in there, and almost in reach but not enough, it's out of reach for now, was the possibility of the box the almighty box, how to get to it might be impossible, the only way would be to come at night without the guide and people.

So the task was on, as day grew into night, later that night they went to the cave with trepidation, got to the tunnel alright and lost their way but Autumns friend stumbled across along with a note saying read, collect this globe and "that's when the guide turned up I knew you lot where been shifty," they looked, astonished to see him and to enquire what he was doing there and what they was doing there it seemed the same thing as him, "no way", yes he once too lived in England, and so took this job on for his future to be able to stop here, so, Autumn begged him and said "it's imperative we find what we are longing and looking for?" That's when he turned round and said "I will help you get the box on condition you have a date with destiny, and she gulped, you're not him are you?" he said "maybe", and a wink, you know, her friends looked on, with curious looks and that's when they came across a very small tunnel, they went to look around that's when they found a globe, in the wall of the cave, never to be moved until this point today, people thought it was stuck in the wall, but the tour guide always said it was and people believed him until now, which meant they were near, in the globe was directions back to the box earlier, to the box the box of destiny and that's when they saw it the box, they scraped, with the stones nearby scraping and scraping until it came free, as it seemed to be well lodged, phew.

It came out of the wall, as it looked like part of the ruins so always kept there with withheld breath Autumn turned the key that she managed to get, she looked at her friends, the globe showed the guide and a love heart, and that when she picked the globe, again showed, in it was a special ring, and when she looked into her globe which was now in the box, she claimed it, it showed a marriage, in the box was trinkets for a marriage too, but in the globe was a mirror, and who it showed was the back of a man's head was it the guide, Mick, or Adam? But the globe lit up, and the guide winked and led them out. He held her hand and whispered in her ear, you will find your true love, but with that, he was gone. "How did he go so quickly?" she said, "He's a magician he's gone."

She and her friends said "Now what? I guess we wait, your destiny is round the corner," They'd didn know why they said it, but she had the globe in her hand showing her wed-ding, and she cried with laughter. She also said I don't think I will go on that date, not a coffee meeting with the vicar. He is too old anyway, and he said he knows me, he lives not far from me I am not interested. Her friend said "yes he is a bit weird why and how did he contact you," the young lad, her friends boyfriend said "well, I think he's trying to find you for some reason maybe just have a coffee see what he wants, let me take you then get you to our home again before you flight back tomorrow, and I will tell you, a story about me, your friend here knows, I nearly got kidnapped, when I was a little boy, he just blurted it out but I will tell you when we are back, what I mean is don't trust anyone, as you can see I am safe but your friend here rescued me a long time ago from someone called Max".

That's when Autumn friend smiled the biggest grin on the planet. He said again I'm safe I am well. And we live here now. I know you will have questions but I am already tracing my family so I can see them, your friend is going to get a job, and live with me", she agreed, she kind of coyly looked and bit her lip "so any time you need to come back you are welcome, in the meantime I'm tracing my mum and dad but we will leave that for another time, she said and "you can visit me, well us and if you need a change of job, we can try get you one you just need to get the right paper work to work here, anyway enough chat for now"

Then silence, was golden all the way to the coffee shop, time to find out what he wanted the vicar.

Later she met with the vicar, yes he did know her and warned her to go back home as Amsterdam is not the right place for her, but as they got talking her bag started to glow, she excused herself and left, the mirror now in her precession, showed the full kidnap of the man her friends boyfriend, wait till she gets home to tell Mr. McKenzie, and ask his proper name too, and flower who did she know what did she know? No, not him she thought not the vicar.

Down on Mesham street, there was still one bank left. All you could see was the rubble near the big vaults, accesses behind the front desk, and down the basement. Sixty minutes had gone by since the CCTV had been cut earlier.

Anne turned to Max, who had hurried across town to meet them, and said, "you turn for a bit, oh hang on, I think I've got it, the safe code." So with sophisticated tools, thanks to Max, the leader, and Frank and the garage owner outside in a nearby sheltered area, talking to himself, mumbling what an idiot he was, but in the at the vaults were Anne to Frank. "Here goes" the mechanical lock used for the safe, the cash box, with the steel door, and strong locks, two clicks to the right, one to the left, then two to the right, "it's wrong," Felix said "two clicks to the right one to the left one the right then two clicks left." See, the garage owner was petrified, in his very last job, old scores did. He is talking to himself again: "why did you agree to be a gateway driver to station point only? Max is taking over from there, thought he had been arrested. Please come so I can go home for tea, and count my money and get my Destiney no more worries, never again, over for good."

The safes were open, another special tool, there is a bit of money with a note with the keys, to open another special box. "It's getting rather hot in here," says Frank. Plus, once this is over, we are done been bullied by you." They waited only ten minutes more, before they had to get out.

The pressure was on; Frank had a go at the safe. They hit something yes there into a box. In the box was one stone, with red on, one big fat jewels and a globe, they took turns to see each other's Destiney, through the globe, chase by police, no, no, we are going to run out of time look again, each had one jewel each, but the globe was glowing Max who seems to be running around like some maniac from one situation across town to another, said give me that here," it showed two people heading to jail, one on the run and one in paradise, oh, so it looked like but couldn't make out who was who, he shouted "let's go lets go now.

They legged it round the back through the basement tunnel out of the bank on to the dark street lit by a tiny street light, then headed onto the getaway car, and that's when the sirens were everywhere, down the streets, it was like a movie, mayhem the vehicle came to a roaring stop while the garage owner opened the door quickly rolls out of the car onto the side of the dark lane, and ran with a hobble into the darkness hiding behind hedges where nobody could see him, hoping not to be involved anymore.

They are shouting at each other whilst Max gets in the driving seat, nearly crashing into the tree but misses as he drives at high speed, the blast of a horn they are driving too fast the car on the other side on the black patchy path, no road markings, the wagon is waving to slow down, as too narrow and they go of the beaten track where do they end but on diggers farm, but at the furthest point possible more into baron land except for a converted unbeknown place the place diggers has a stick made like a crutch in his hand again as he only just escaped, near death himself, it was covered in mud made worse when the police start chasing the others. Digger going mental at them, they were going round and round then and almighty crash into Diggers new funny dwelling, smashed up with broken glass everywhere Max ran off not hurt, with the police trying to catch him, but he is fast on his feet.

But who's left with injuries but Frank and Anne, followed by the police reading them the rights and saying you're both under arrest? An ambulance was called for Digger and the others, but the police need a word with Digger too. Followed by a weary Kev, who had been in the other car on the other side of the road before the wagon had stopped to see what was happening, he was trying to find out, about his mum and scrambling to the floor. He told the ambulance, "I waiting a long time for his mum, hoping to come to her rescue, but she had got lost and all that bad weather." She is out there and that's when I drove the car and came here, she had called earlier that day." Max was on the run sirens everywhere, In the corner of a field was Desis wife counting money from an open box, and police surrounding the place, and nowhere to run.

Who was in the wagon on a hunt for a box were Jenny, Charley, Adam and the good doctor was driving, as he actually owns the wagon, well it's his brother who was Adam, who had mentioned Autumn which led them to meet up with the others again wishing to meet up with Autumn at some point. Adam used the truck for special events truck and wagon events, in a panic over the other drivers which the doctor had collapsed at the wheel, and Charley suddenly grabbed the wheel next thing we know is was beep, beep, beep the machines were driving them nuts with the hospital staff, looking on telling them they had boxes under their trolleys besides them but the contents kept in a safe at the hospital they could get their possessions after their hospital treatments the good Dr himself needed tests urgently. He had a mini-stroke with all the commotion. The cold sweat and feeling sick did not help with the police outside the door.

Sally, Bob and Jay, found themselves in a difficult situation. Jay managed to catch up with the others, they all felt stressed and lost. They could not navigate their way back home without any signal on their devices. They realized they were in a precarious position, regretting their decision to climb that hill. Despite having a map, they misinterpreted its instructions. Their initial mistake was entering the woods first, which was a wrong move. Furthermore, Bobs choice to take out the map during bad weather resulted in it getting caught on a branch. While trying to retrieve it. Jay accidently tore the map. Although they had a rough idea of where to head next, they had completely lost their sense of direction.

Would they ever reach their intended destination?

"What a stupid thing this is; why did we agree to do this in this weather?" Sally said, and jay turned round said

"Because we want our treasure, wait till I get my hands on that teacher." They walked aimlessly through the days cold, trying to make sense of it all. They needed to rest from the cold chill, so begin searching for a much warmer place to rest for now. Bob, Sally, and Jay, and all friends now, were heading for one nice outcome. Still, they were stuck a hill trying to relocate their steps. But, as to was getting late, they had to try get to a point where they would be safe. There is no way here on the map. They think they made out a little shelter in a cave. When the weather turns a bit drier they can move on. They had a few supplies with them, and so could at least eat for now, it was starting to get to the warm shelter and try to huddle together, but they looked at the map and they are could just about make out where they needed to be, hopefully and then they can get there boxes to hopefully paradise.

A few hours later, looking all bedraggled, they went on a hunted to the river and down past the cliffs to the little hut at the end of the bay. Praying the boxes were there, they attentively opened the door to the hut with a bit of a push almost fell through the door, as it was a bit stuck.

They relaxed for a minute in some chairs, it looked like someone lived there, with a cup and plate on the side, but they just needed a dry place for now, plus the directions, if they had it right, they would be here. They will get dry and fathom out why they are here. And why would their boxes be here? They have never been here before, which they don't recall as kids.

Mrs. B had escaped everyone and clawed her way through the mud, because she had slipped again. She heard the sound of a hound, thought it was brave; she knew she found him before, but didn't know he had gone. He must have tried to get help, or hoping someone would recognize the dog, and bravely bring them to her, and she just lay there. The rain had stopped at least, and her breath went up and down. She was tired and shut her eyes, trying to be brave in her pain and rest, she remembered where the box could be because when she was little, this is what happened.

Her mum and dad, at the time, took her to some old lodges next to Diggers' land, and when she remembered, that fun day with her dad and the special key that was given to her as a present to keep, she now remembers where the map was. Once she can hobble there now its dry, she can get to her destiny. The barking gets louder, and louder, with rescue from a stranger, who asked before you take me to hospital, please can I collect a box, "I will pay you,"

the stranger said. "No need I will take you. You will have what you need." she looked all glazed over. Still, she knew she would get what she needed a new home for her brave and the cats. She knew she would be ok, and she just smiled, ok handsome, take me to paradise. She surprised herself saying that but she just had to say it.

Chapter Six

MR. MCKENZIE, FLOWER, AND the caretaker, had to find the other box. Flower had got a phone call to say to meet, at the beck near the teacher Mr. McKenzie. In the meantime, he thought back he remembered this is his memory.

When he was younger, he remembered been friends with a girl much younger than him, and she used to wear flowers in her hair, and in fact looked a bit like flower. He checked with her yes; it was her, so he thought, and he remembered an older, wiser older teenager at the park.

They were playing together, and formed a lasting friendship this been this boy now the caretaker, told them what his mother had said "when you get older you will be the chosen person, and as you do, you will laugh it off, until one day a person will give you a special box and keys to give out, and they laughed some more, the caretakers mother was from far and had travelled many miles to find him and his little friends, and all of a sudden he came out of his trance like state when the caretaker said "do you remember we was playing we got told that in years to come the box of interest will be at the beck, when he was in fact the keeper where time is kept". They all laughed long ago.

Autumn, had a phone call to meet there, when they got to the beck, they knew all four were connected and they told have to find the box of destiny. Mr. McKenzie had wondered why he had recognized flower that first meeting. It was fate, they had lost contact due to the fact she had moved away and now back as a teacher. Mr. McKenzie, his real name was John, she chatted to him at school he knew she would be a teacher, in fact he had not only been entrusted with the keys and the keeper of time, he needed his little warrior gang this time united to collect all the keys after everyone's destiny, he could go back to solve mysteries, and they can conquer there owns fears and conquer peoples desires and bring them forth and now too much just for him and his helper the caretaker he needed help from the band of four, so they all held hands, and united again never to lose their friendship again, and decided to go on a very big digging session by the beck.

The caretaker, who wasn't very clever, took a handkerchief from his pocket. Only what had landed, was stripes of paper that he had forgotten to put there. He was nearly going to lie, but then explained why he had them. He couldn't write very well; this was his way of getting people to help him. He, too, had been told years ago by his mother. When Autumn arrived and put her hand over her eyes, wiped down her Face, and asked, "Why didn't you say I can teach you, and so can I said? "Flower chimed in, saying, so can I." Flower also wondered how people they haven't seen had gotten along and how other people found out about their box. Now we know. Later that day, Jay, Sally and Bob gathered around to open the box.

Sally discovered an old leather-bound book of facts and strongly desired to return to college, seeing it as a sign.

Jay found matchstick and a letter indicating the opportunity to have his place. Having forgiven Jay, Bob realized that holding onto their grudge was pointless. He examined his puzzle item, which seemed to hold his destiny, according to a note inside. Despite his best efforts, Bob struggled to open the puzzle, but Jay opened the puzzle, but Jay effortlessly opened it in an instant. This frustrated Bob, but it revealed images of animals and a farm, symbolizing new beginnings.

Bob could vividly envision the farm as he closed his eyes, realizing that achieving it would require passing certain stages and seeking Jays assistance. This would allow Jay to have his place as well, with the condition of maintaining a distance from Sally. However, the situation took an unexpected turn when the police stormed place where Sally was, leading to her arrest. Everyone was shocked, their eyes wide and mouths agape. Despite the upheaval, Sally smiled and reassured them, saying "It's okay. We will have that farm, but not yet."

Sometime later

Headline news, owners wife arrested, for attempted murder of a child, turns out although wasn't actual killer, but she nearly killed a child because she was so upset that she couldn't have children, and when she was with Jay she thought she was invisible and he had talked her out of killing just because she couldn't have children and told her the whole affair was wrong, she apparently had a funny going on with her own mother and father that didn't care for her much she wanted a child and she got so angry, she nearly killed a child and got blamed the mystery still unknown until she found herself looking at plane walls and in a hospital bed and a nurse looking over concern that she hadn't eaten or drank much, and was now been tube fed until she progresses, after having an attack, but she will get help, with her anger issues, the clinical smell the cleanliness all too familiar from childhood, when the good doctor came to see her to annualize her mental state and she is to be sectioned, and when she is ready to tell about what she saw then, when she is better mentally they will consider letting her free until then she has a few years of recovery. And that was the case for the squad of four to uncover the real killer.

Further, Charley, Adam, and Jenny, and Ron tried to find their powerful box, which they had been digging in the dried-up mud to find something hard-not, only a stone, but crunch, what was it? Wait, Jenny found the edge of the box; they pulled it out, unlocked the box, and a whole haze came out, a sort of whirling dust. They followed the dust to a little old barn. They heard funny noises coming from the corridor they ran out, and said "If that's our destination it can wait. And they all laughed.

Further Down at a different location were John McKenzie, Flower, Autumn, and the caretaker named Bill, now on their new mission, detectives, keeper of keys, and Destiney, whatever lures behind doors or passages, mysteries to solve next mission Destiney awaits.

THE END

JANET BAILEY

BLACKPOOL

A BIZARRE TALE

BLACKPOOL, A BIZARRE TALE

Chapter One

Lucy, Edna, Mia, and Zane formed a group of school friends and computer enthusiasts. They were joined by Mary, accompanied by two older kids named Josh and Anne, as well as her husband Carl. Aunt Wendy, her cleaner Mrs. Binglow, and gardener Jeff also joined the gathering. Cheryl and her boyfriend, along with driver Dan and Sally, were part of the group, along with Jenny and two older teenagers. Among the passengers were Lily and Tom, and finally, the elderly lady, Mrs. Bing. The last to join were Rose and Eddy, who served as the landlord and landlord of the local public house.

Blackpool trip encounters the bizarre tale.

Those stupid bullies from school. "no, I'm not going to answer them," she thought in her head, but then said, "They want us to go to the school reunion." She looked with desperate eyes at her dear old friend, Edna, also from school. "I am looking forward to our trip to Blackpool, aren't you Edna? At the weekend, time to think about the school get-together, or not? I'm not sure, even though I don't know if we should go?" "How on earth did they track us down? It's been sixty years," "It would have been nice to see the other two of our little geeky club friends, Mia, and our only good-looking male friend, Zane. What a whizz kid on computers, along with Mia; she was bright.

I think there on social media we could contact them, see what they are up to, now, I hope if we go, although I doubt it because we don't want to see the bullies, you know what, we had the best time back then, despite them idiots. Well, on top of that, I have had enough of my husband trying to control me." "Oh, Lucy, did you get more money for our trip? And you're so strong now, listen to you, and glad you told me he is away at a conference; it's your only chance". "I know Edna, you're not going to believe it, but the last couple of months I managed to get money from his wallet, he has been so drunk every week it was like it was heaven sent finally. However, I had to hide it, and I mean really hide it. He thought he had spent it. He has given me freedom this weekend because he thinks I'm babysitting the grandkids, finally one whole weekend; this is my first reprieve in years." She thought to herself, she may not come back.

Back in the old town was Mary and her two kids, one boy and one girl, her husband Carl, is working away but will meet them there at her so-called Aunts, well a woman wrote to them from Blackpool, claiming to be a lost Aunt, Aunt Wendy she even writes letters to her two teenage children, Josh and Anne all very exciting they cannot wait to go and see what she is like, by all accounts she has loads of rooms in her old fashioned house with creaky walls and doors, sometimes she jokes she has ghosts.

She says its unique qualities; she says it's got mysterious and a bit chilly, so bring jumpers and bare floorboards that creak along with the staircases and whistling at the windows, but the kids, although anxious, love all that and want to investigate her Attic as they in-teresting things their dad been an archaeologist, and also into the paranormal.

Mary was doing her family tree, and her husband wasn't too sure about this Aunt, but it was a little trip away for her and the kids; many people believe in ghosts. "So there are things that go bump in the night," said her Aunt. Well, they will go and see what awaits them; with apprehension and the bags packed, they are ready to rumble.

Having to live as a dead person becomes the last thing Cheryl wants. The last time she was talking and alive was with her boyfriend. He drives coaches for a living. Where do angels go when they die? What do angels do when they die if they know they will be reincarnated? She wondered is that me? Hang on a minute. Are there nurses around my hospital bed? A coma? Are you insane? I'm alive. I'm here, look. "I'm talking to you. Hey, aren't you listening, hey nurse, why are you not answering me?" With pitting looks from the nurses going about their normal lives, little machines going off, activities are a bit frantic tonight, not enough staff, "Hey, can anyone hear me? I'm here; why? What happened to me?"

The moment she walked by and saw a man sobbing, what's going on? Dan, her boyfriend? It's been weeks now, but he regained his position at work. He needs to keep busy and earn a living. One more day and the trip to Blackpool is here. He was wondering what sort of passengers he would have. He will see Cheryl on the way back again. "sorry, love, I have to work." He couldn't believe Cheryl was in hospital. He could not take any more time off but promised to see her after this trip. Maybe they could have a trip together somewhere warm when she was well again. "Dan, Dan, can you hear me? Oh, I see, ignore me. I only wanted to see If you were okay. I've never seen you cry before." She took herself away from the situation. Oh, fair enough. Talk to you when you're calm."

"I can see myself. Wait, how can I be there on the bed yet walk to see Dan crying.! I'm not going to be hysterical aaaaaahhhhhhh".

In Meadow Valley Were Sally and Jenny, the two older teenagers who had never been to Blackpool before, or so they thought. They were backpacking and going to stop in hostels for an adventure like no other. Their parents trusted them, but they had to keep in contact. It was a big thing to let them go. They had completed college and were still young, but they wanted to experience something and places before going to real jobs and real commitments.

They laughed at almost everything and were a real joy to be around. They joked about going to a commune, but that did not go well. They have been friends forever. Sally plays guitar, and Jenny sings so they can busk if they run out of money. The main thing is Jenny's dad and Sally's dad quietly put money into their accounts for emergencies. They are all friends but dare not tell the mums it's their secret. Blackpool, here we come, all packed and ready. Today, the girls kept getting Deja vu moments as if they had made this journey before. They had old clippings in their rucksacks as they had been looking up their family tree and other information.

When they got to a hostel, they spent some days going through them and looking around Blackpool, exploring and maybe seeing if it has much history. They wondered where they should start. They knew that, in 1879, some electric lights were switched on in Blackpool. At that time, electric light was very new and exciting, and the event attracted many visitors. An electric tramway opened in Blackpool in 1885. In 1889, the Opera House was built.

South Pier opened in 1893. Blackpool is famous for its tower. Blackpool Tower was built between 1891 and 1894.

North Promenade was built in the years 1893-1899. The older Promenade was widened in the years 1903-1905.

So, they will try to find a museum, plus they heard a couple of the old pubs have history, maybe they can venture into one or two. All for a good cause, of course. The girls laughed at this thought as they both said it. "Let's have a cuppa first before we go anywhere. It is nice to relax a bit first. I hope we have everything we need, Sally; do you remember your bank card? You may laugh, but you lost it that time by the river, all wet and muddy and looked funny and mucky, and that was a palaver trying to find it at the edge. Because you fell in and then had to cancel your card till you got another, you looked like a girl been through a hedge backward." "Cheeky, but yes, I have it safe, and you?" then, as usual, giggling with Jenny making impressions of Sally looking like that. "Wait, it's your turn next time." Then they laughed some more. Warming their hands around their hot drinks. Although they weren't cold, it was just all the excitement. Jenny's dad said,

"Hope you're both well; keep safe for you and Sally. Your dad says to be careful, mums do too, but all-knowing, in fact, Jenny, your mum is here now don't worry Sally, love your mums working she will ring you later Sally okay love." "Yes, I know I spoke to her first; she said she would ring Later."

Sally and Jenny had known each other forever. Although they are both single, they eventually want to find love. As kids, they said they would marry each other if they didn't find anyone by age thirty. However, they said they wanted to date boys, so they went out with two lads after school, but they were only eighteen years old, so there was plenty of time. The lads couldn't understand their friendship, so they left both of them. They needed to find a better boyfriend. Maybe people like them; it was a friendship like a marriage, but they might find love soon. The funny thing is they feel like this Deja vu thing is real every time they see young men or places they have not been to before, and they get feelings like they have been. How strange is that? The excitement is building one more sleep, and they go in the morning. They couldn't wait to check and re-check their bags, money notes pad, electric devices, and bank cards.

Aunt Wendy is setting everything up, helping to make everything she needs to be right. She hadn't entertained in ages, turning down the corners of the sheets and having the toilet roll edges to fine art, but she has a cleaner, Mrs. Binglow, and just goes over the finer details herself.

Aunt Wendy knows exactly what she wants and aims to get it. She told Mrs. Binglow she could go home early, but she would still pay her and see her next week, but if she needed her before, she would call her. Same with the gardener, Jeff, the garden was spot on. He does wonders with the trees, making fun shapes. She loved all that stuff; she was a bit stuck up, but she had a fun side regarding her garden. She liked quirky trees, and an old oak tree had been made into an old-fashioned tree house that her dad had done years ago.

She was an old bird but still fit, but under that tough exterior, she actually did have a heart but forgotten how to use her heart for good. Her legs might not be able to climb the ladders to the tree house as well as she did, but if she needed to, she would climb, even if a bit cumbersome.

She knew the tree house needed repair but didn't find the need to repair it just yet. Even though it's been attacked by the elements over the years, and the wood is starting to splinter and rot, she knows that the gardener will fix it soon. He's a good soul. The other side of the garden has a tool shed, but she is sure the Gardner goes in there to have a quiet drink on his break. She hasn't sacked him because she likes him. He is a gentle soul and good at his job. She nearly did sack him but then actually decided to leave it. He's been there twenty years now and very reliable, mainly the odd time he seemed cheeky as ever.

The sun was very low in the sky, but dark clouds formed as the group gathered around the coach, excitement buzzing. They were all set for their adventure—a journey that promised beautiful landscapes, laughter, and new-found friendships. But little did they know that fate had other plans. As the group boards the coach, they notice an unfamiliar face. A mysterious stranger claims to be part of the trip, but nobody remembers inviting them. This secret stranger drops hints about hidden secrets and a shared past throughout the journey. Who was he? And what connection do they have to the group? Dan thought he recognized him, but with his beard, he looked a bit different, although he thought he knew him somehow.

As the coach winds through picturesque landscapes, tensions rise within the group. One of the travelers is an undercover agent tasked with sabotaging the trip, or so the passengers thought, because people noticed he was fidgeting and kept looking back. Who would betray them?

The passengers clung to each other as the coach hurtled down winding roads. They laughed; they were puzzled and wondered what was going on. He engaged in hushed conversations and exchanged messages with unknown contacts. At the back of the bus, the last-minute bookings like his as he wasn't on from the beginning. Only time would reveal the truth.

The two women. Lucy and Edna sat in front of the coach.

Lucy's eyes held secrets. Whilst Dan, with skepticism and curiosity as to why his friend wanted to see him later, is the one they call Wendy. Their purpose was to meet this woman too, but Lucy had strange contents in her bag she would have to sort when Dark, Dan on the other hand, had been asked if people wanted to see the clairvoyant Wendy, who had remained hard to track down for years.

As the coach rolled along the coast, he thought about Cheryl, "Hello Dan," "What? who said that!" It's me, Cheryl, "he nearly crashed the coach looking for her; the other passengers had travelled with him before, so they hired him and asked what he was doing, and the stranger just laughed. Dan said, "Was that you pretending to be Cheryl," no, I'm laughing because you are asking people to see a clairvoyant, a friend of yours now; you're talking to yourself," "Well, who are you? These people are good customers. Who are you?" "Well, I booked with you," "I don't remember that. The person who makes the bookings didn't say this is a small coach for a few people. Yes, we have a few others I don't know, but I do know half a dozen of the passengers, and well, you look." he broke his sentence off and carried on to for a pit stop whilst the others got off to go to the restrooms so they can finish their last leg of the journey oh so they think.

Mary and her family began their road trip to Blackpool, and anticipation hung. The woman claiming to be their aunt had sent messages hinting at long-lost secrets and hidden connections. The children chattered excitedly in the backseat. While Mary was curious, she opened the letters. At the much-needed coffee break, letters from the woman claiming to be their aunt and a clairvoyant would arrive in mysterious rose-colored envelopes; each letter would be carefully handwritten. They were on their way now, and she knew Carl would meet her the next day.

They could have the clairvoyant night, which meant one thing the kids could be left, hopefully, to do what they do best and investigate: They were proper little private investigators. They were that from a young investigating everything, including even the food, in case there was something they didn't like which made the parents laugh.

Bob is a middle-aged man with a grudge. For years, he toiled as a driver for the same company, the small business shuttling tourists to Blackpool's glittering attractions. But beneath his courteous smile lay bitterness—

the kind that festers when dreams are crushed Certainly, and Dan recognized him now. He lost his job because he was poorly, and Dan got his job, not unintentionally. It just happened Bob left coded notes in the restroom stalls.

"Unlock the door," they read. The passengers, intrigued and slightly unnerved, followed the clues but said, "Stop this cloak and dagger stuff. It's me; it's not my fault you weren't well. I heard you had a breakdown, and I'm sorry you lost your wife. I recognize you; we met when I got the job and you were leaving.

Please don't take it out on my passenger and me. You can chat with us. You're amongst friends, not enemies.

Suddenly, it became a little darker, and although Dan had done this trip before, hoping he wouldn't hear voices again, the trees started to sway in the wind, and the little coach stopped. They panicked a bit as the signals went off with the bad weather and people trying desperately to get a signal, as it seemed like a thunderstorm was brewing. They were not far from Blackpool now, but they had to get to safety and had to wait for any oncoming traffic so that they could call the breakdown number. In the meantime, they had to connect and form a bond whilst they waited and waited; this felt like forever, even though it wasn't that long.

When help arrived in the form of Bing on her way home from seeing her trusted friend and heading for Blackpool The rain drumming against the windows of the little coach, its wheels had already sunk a bit into the mud. The passengers, a motley crew of customers bound for Blackpool, exchanged worried glances. The driver had announced that they were stranded due to a signal failure. The storm outside raged on, lightning splitting the sky.

Outside the coach in her car came to a halt sat a little old lady, Mrs. Bing, as she announced to them her silver hair was neatly pinned, and her eyes sparkled with mischief.

She clutched her worn handbag, which held secrets older than the hills. Mrs Bing had seen her fair share of storms and knew this was different.

Panic began to creep through the coach as the minutes stretched into hours. People fidgeted, checked their phones still (no signal), and whispered about missed connections and ruined holidays. But Mrs Bing remained calm. She had a plan. She had a signal on and off, so she had to wait.

Mrs Bing knew the ex-employee would be here trying to sabotage the coach, "come on, son, you know you cannot do it", she said, "you have a new job now caring for me. He said, "You don't need to care for me. Oh yes, I do. I might get into mischief, and you will get paid. It won't be much, but you can live back with me." then Dan gasped, "Oh yes, you were our boss before Cheryl took over, but we have a stand-in person until she comes out of the hospital, "Yes, Dan that's right." was a voice "what, what how you talking to me." Everyone looked as if he was mad, and he said I could hear Cheryl, and they looked at him like he was mad, Mrs Bing with her sensible shoes squeaking on the wet floor. Dan said, "Look, have you got a signal. We're stuck,"

Mrs Bing smiled sweetly. "Oh, I think there's a way, dear.

You see, I've got a little secret." She pulled a watch from her bag but said, "watch carefully; she wasn't joking. She twisted the watch's dial, and suddenly, the rain ceased, and the thunder hushed. But she had already called for help, but they hadn't seen her. Don't think it was a miracle, even though her signal was going on and off like the others.

The coach jolted forward only after they had been rescued, and as time went on, the passengers gasped as they saw the familiar Blackpool Tower in the distance.

As the coach rolled into Blackpool, Mrs. Bing's plan un-folded. She met them there and directed the driver to a small café near the promenade. The passengers filed out, still dazed from the sudden change in weather. They made it. The funny thing was it was a friend of hers that owned the cafe, but to be honest, they weren't bothered, they were glad to stop so that they could venture to their accommodation or some stopped in hostels and just arranged for the transport back with Dan, He was there as a driver for them it wasn't an escorted tour. Still, he had arranged for some people to see the so-called clairvoyant Wendy, and others just wanted to see the sites. It was a very small group.

Chapter Two

Finally, the family arrived at Aunt Wendy's. Josh and Anne are very excited to be at Aunt Wendy's, for one reason only to see if anything is interesting in the Attic and to see what creepy noises they can hear, no sleeping with one eye open. She showed them to three rooms; one of them had a large, old-fashioned and high bed. The first thing the kids did was bounce on the beds in each of the three rooms. Their rooms had twin beds, old-fashioned beds next door to each other, and some old toys with an old-fashioned draw for clothes. But on further investigation, Anne put her hand under the draw, which seemed to lead to a secret compartment. She didn't say anything as the others were leaving them in the room; she would look properly soon.

The next day, it meant they could sneak up to the Attic, whilst the others would be on their clairvoyant evening, and a few more from the coach trip were coming, so a little gathering and that meant one thing: Wendy had notification from the coach that others were coming to see her tomorrow, for a clairvoyant night.

That very night after arriving the front door creaked open, revealing a dimly lit hallway. Dust was everywhere; where was the cleaner? Footsteps echoed as they climbed the narrow staircase. The air grew colder, and the wooden steps; when shown up the stairs to the bedroom, they knew the way now because yesterday it was cold and creepy, but just past that was the Attic. They were definitely going to investigate; they did wait for the dad to arrive later that day and told him to meet them at the Attic; later, he showed them how to get the steps down to the Attic and told the others that the kids were just doing their own thing as after all they were young teenagers.

Then, as they turned the handle towards them, the windows were covered with paper, and the air smelled of mothballs and decay. Even though Mrs. Binglow comes to clean, she won't come here.

The floorboards creaked under Anne's and Josh's trainers.

The room seemed smaller than it should be. Maybe there are some hidden walls, they hoped. In one corner stood an ancient rocking chair, its wood worn down a bit; it swayed gently as if remembering lost occupants. Then stopped rocking, which was very scary, which made the kids scream, wondering if dad could hurry up. It was a bit creepy, but they put on brave faces to face their fears of the unknown, As Josh explored, he found an old trunk in the room. Inside lay yellowed letters, brown stained photographs, of two girls that he had met once before at the booking office of the coach, but his Mum decided to drive to Wendy's instead, and then he saw it—a name etched into the trunk's lid. It wasn't Wendy's. They knew they would have to investigate tomorrow if dad didn't hurry up.

Further uptown, the two older teenage girls Sally and Jenny, who got on well with Lily and Tom, stopped at the same hostel and coincidence was they were doing some investigations into their past, so Sally and Jenny told them about the clippings and Tom and Lily they told them about archives and a library that they could take them too but for now just to get food and bed. Sally giggled to Jenny before bed. Maybe we can go to the pub for lunch and be grown up, which sets them off giggling. "Yes, well, we are just old enough."

Sally and Jenny decide it's a good idea to go along with Lily and Tom. They are a couple of years older, and this is their second trip here; they did one last year to Bruges, but they know they have to do normal jobs at some point but asked if they wanted to busk with them for a few hours before going to the library, "Yes we are then doing our first gig at the local pub," As they know the landlord they are welcome to come along. They said, "Who knows, maybe you can do that one day. I see you have a guitar with you," "Yes, I do, and Sally sings." What a coincidence. That's when they headed out, and as they were walking, Jenny had flashbacks about four people that looked like four people in a band that looked like them. But she didn't know if it was just a strange dream even though she was awake, and had to sit down very quickly and told of her sudden dream, very unearthing they were stopping there anyway, to busk but then the others had to sit down and retold of Déjà vu, that they have had, so after busking for money, they let Lilly and to Tom keep more of the money explaining they are helping them. They knew their dads were helping them. However, they need to earn money for themselves; eventually, they will.

Sometime later, after looking through the archives, they have very real experience they saw themselves, and with horrified faces, they immediately they wanted to see the Librarian who is in charge of the archives only to find to they have to come back first thing in the morning, they definitely would need a drink now, when they got to the pub the landlady rose and her partner Eddy to greet Tom and lily but when Sally came back from the ladies Rose went white, started whispering all four of them the pictures on the wall looked like them, and they asked what was wrong and pointed to the picture, and Sally and Jenny went a ghastly white too, asking why they had their picture of them in a band from years ago, and Eddy left the room abruptly only to come back with a photo album, but come back tomorrow or after they had entertained there customers to reveal more about the photos, but first to serve the customers and Tom and Lily did their turn singing, and got the crowds singing along, it turned out a very good first gig.

The photos are now very old but show them in old clothes but also of them being younger, leading to an unfinished mission with the help of the landlady and landlord of the pub. Each photo tells the story, but the last page has a handwritten letter to her children, Mrs. Bing. And where to find her if she's in Blackpool? It has something to do with a missing watch that needs to go back to where it belongs in the ruins on a map to a place called High Acre Rocks.

The artefact needs to go back so they can go back, but the rest was unreadable, and back where? Where to find her? A quest for tomorrow after the library.

The day after Mia and Zane heard from the old school friends via social media, they just about managed to try to track them down; with a few people helping along the way, they heard news about the school reunion from Lucy and Edna. They, too, didn't want to see the bullies but did want the reunion of friends from their geeky club. They would be happy to see them. They reminisced about one day from school that sent shudders down the arms of Mia and Zane and said "Do you remember that awful day, all can say is I'm glad the bullies got suspended" Zane said, "it was awful there were you me Sally and Jenny when we got tricked I cannot even say their names without cringing, we had all got detention, because we were using the computers in school without permission." Mia said "yes and the bullies were in trouble but they wouldn't let us pass, and starting calling us geeky, and useless at sports and no good, then they took it too far and tried to drag you to the toilet and we were all shouting at dragging you back, until the caretaker stopped them and Lucy and Edna had already encountered them earlier, with their taunts that's why they were in detention, but we survived."

"Yes, we did and we are alive, I'm not sure about going to the reunion, but I'm happy to meet out lovely friends, it's been ages." "yes we can see what their up to and take it from there, I do miss them," "We both do." So, they had been working abroad for years and came back to England to see friends; they decided to get in contact again with Lucy and Edna and decided to see where they are now, and they could come and see them. Lucy replied on their behalf and told them they were in Blackpool.

Lucy left a note for Edna on the bed, revealing a confession. The note instructed Edna to meet her at the seafront if she wanted to discover what was in her bag, or else they could meet later. Confused, Edna initially thought it was just a walk. After hurrying along and nearly exhausting herself, she found Lucy on the beach, braving the blustery day.

Shouting to get Lucy's attention, Edna finally made her way to her friend. Lucy, seemingly lost in thought, had something in her bag. Peering inside, Edna was taken aback to see what looked like ashes in a plastic bag. As Lucy stood and walked towards the water, Edna rushed to catch up, demanding an explanation. Lucy cryptically said, "This is him." Bewildered, Edna questioned, "Him? Your husband?"

Before Edna could react, the ashes were released into the sea. Mouth gaping open, Edna had countless questions racing through her mind. Had he died? Did she cremate him? Was Lucy on the run from the police? Beads of sweat formed on Edna's brow as she sternly demanded, "You better explain, Lucy, right now!" Clearly agitated, Lucy struggled to stand firm. Edna repeated, her voice sharp,

"Explain now." Lucy began to share, "The other week, he didn't trust me. He doubted my sincerity about our grandchildren." She paused, gazing into space, leaving Edna to ponder the complex situation.

"Dan, Dan, you need to go to Wendy's house; something's not right."

"What? How are you talking to me?"

"I think through telepathy, Dan. Wendy's, she's up to no good.

No time to explain, but you know I got knocked out and ended up in a coma. I just found out. God, I hope I can get out of it because I discovered that the policeman was working with Mary to cover up. She's not a clairvoyant; she's fake and the head of a money laundering ring. My ex-husband, with the help of the crooked policeman, is watching over me. He told the nurses he was waiting for me to wake up. Now I'm stuck here, but she was..." and then it went quiet.

"Cheryl, come back! Tell me what you were going to say."

All he could do was wait and wait and go to Wendy's house. First, a visit to the police, but he realized he would sound mad, and they might take him away to be sectioned. He couldn't' take that chance until he knew more.

So, he cautiously went to the police station with hesitation, but he had to try to make sense of it. Praying that he didn't sound mentally unstable hearing voices, Cheryl was keeping him company on his journey to the police station, even though it looked like he was talking to himself. Shouting out, "Please be quiet for a minute while I think." That's when the policeman said, "How can I help you?"

Chapter Three

Mrs. Bing was off to see her long-lost sister, and with the help of a private investigator, he managed to locate Mrs. Binglow; she managed to get to the location easily through the click of the old watch; it was found in High Acres Rock this is her tale going back.

Mrs. Bing's name is Jen, and Mrs. Binglow Mel had gone on an adventure to High Acres Rock, a secluded little spot with green spots of moss, a small quantity of wildlife, and chirping birds in the background. Not much going on, and only a tiny cave nearby with a few high rocks, some too dangerous and high to climb, which attract the odd visitor now and again, but one day, before heading to the rocks, there was a watchmaker in the small town who was mending a watch and told them it could lead to the past and present. However, the other watch had gone missing on his walk, so the girls offered to help him find it in exchange for keeping one of them temporarily to see if it worked. If they found it, he was reluctant. He said, "If you find it, you can borrow it for your adventure, but you must bring it back." Jen (Mrs. Bing) must take it back but hasn`t yet; Mrs. Bing must take it to the watchmaker, as consequences and rules.

The watch has a secret mechanism that allows the wearer to twist the dial to travel through time, only Jen can't take it back straight away until she knows what happened to her sister's kids and the watchmaker's kids so they can go back to the watchmaker and give it to him, but that lead to a curse because they hadn't headed straight back after their adventure, but that meant instead when Mel (Mrs. Binglow) the cleaner lost her children through time, and that's where the story of the four older teenagers, are now finding out from the library photos and the photos in the bar why they needed to find a Mrs. Binglow there mother. How do we put the universe back together as one, somewhere along the time continuum, where the past was now in the present? This left Mrs. Binglow lonely and with no children and no sister because as they clicked the watch, only one travelled through time, that was Jen (Mrs. Bing), helping others along the way but now finally, after years, found the house she was cleaning at a Lady's house apparently she was called Wendy. The last name is unknown; the private investigator will let her know further information as it comes in. Now, to knock at that door.

The bar was steady with a small stream of customers, and who should be in it was Dan. He had caught up with Mrs Bing and would meet with Wendy later. He had to ask Rose or Eddy if they knew much about Mary, and then he began to tell him about the four people, who had a tremendous shock about their mother and for his ears only Eddy said to come in the back room, whilst he told him what he knew as follows.

Apparently, down at High Acres Rock this is what was told four children had gone missing, apparently; they had travelled and been stuck in a time loop that they couldn't get out of, but accidentally, Jen had clicked the watch in her pocket, but she had finally put the watch back at High Acres Rock, but before she did this is what happened, that repurchased the kids, they kept getting that Deja vu, they broke the loop but this is what happened when they were away.

They had met up with four other travelers with similar experiences over the years. What happened was that these people were lost in time. They all got back by the click of some watches, but apparently, the watchmaker's kids had stumbled across this magnificent watch.

"Look here," they said, "what's our dad working on? The watch looks fascinating." That's when they had gone into a time loop. When Mrs. Bing returned, he wanted her to return their children, but time was sensitive. She had been too long putting it back the first time, at the rocks, but will be placing the watch back this week and taking it to the old watchmaker.

In the meantime, the kids were at the central point in Parkville, not far from the rocks, but they didn't know where they were. They crossed over the rocks and came across some old buildings. They approached the office building; there didn't seem to be anyone around. They tried the door with apprehension, and it opened automatically, but nobody was about until they heard rustling noises.

As the other two had already been in the building, running around until Jenny fell into a door leading to a lab, it got bizarre. The others followed and were in danger if they didn't find a way back. They didn't have a watch; they explained when they calmed down after asking a million questions because they knew them.

They had been stuck in this loop of déjà vu for months or years; they didn't know. They had one watch that had stopped working, but somewhere in the lab, there must be parts. But then, they realized they were stuck here until they figured it out. They were all trapped, and the watch was, in fact, not just a time machine but another type of device. In fact, they found notes, and the other two had been trying to get it fixed because they knew it would bring them back.

The computer came on and off; they had been trying for so long and feeling they had been watched when a voice came from nowhere, saying, "It worked, yes, it worked,"

which freaked them out. "Where was the voice coming from?" Trying not to panic, Sally heard the voice, just her this time. Cheryl explained she was called Cheryl and was trying to return to her body. She explained to tap the computer now that they had been lost souls, but they had been reincarnated into these bodies.

Just as they were about to get information from the computer, it stopped working, and they had to follow the computer's system to get released to get the parts for their watch. If they succeeded, in their heads, they would be let go. If not, they would be stuck in the past. They needed to get the right bit for the watch to get to safety, or at least to the other room where there were vending machines with food and drinks. They could click the eye to safety when they found the parts from the clues, with everyone pulling as a team and not screaming at each other. They were unlocking the clues bit by bit. One of the clues was that Mrs.

Binglow originally worked for some science people, but she left in a hurry. She had got the job as an investigator, and investigating all the evidence was there for them to unlock the reality. The universe could be one again, and they got to go home once they fixed the watch.

After hours of following clues and reading about their mother and the watchmaker, they knew both had worked there and left quickly.

Still, the only thing left was the bits of the watch to find the mechanism, and then they would be back to the present day, and an explanation that finally the clock had been put back by Mrs. Bing and that the watchmakers had separate watches along with his children. All four children had thought of died years ago but had disappeared through time; with Cheryl's voice leading them to the right place and the click of the watch, they were there outside Wendy's along with Dan, and Cheryl had almost completed her mission to wake up.

Chapter Four

THE CLAIRVOYANT NIGHT AND Cheryl were talking to Dan as he entered the steps of Wendy's house; a whole host of people and unexpected guests; although Wendy had plans, she established that these people had somehow turned up at her front door, the gardener had turned quickly upon her request to help her get everyone settled for her clairvoyant night, she was going to make a lot more money than expected, she was dubious how others that were not invited came, but Dan said "there from my little coach, and not to worry it was all in hand," he had a glint in his eyes and a wide smile that relaxed her, they had just started with the help of Jeff, the gardener if he wanted to keep his job to do exactly what she wants and a pay rise, he complied for now.

John and Anne had investigated the secret space in her draw and found some mysterious key; they had now time to open that trunk in the loft; they presumed with excitement that this was the key to that mysterious trunk, they were already in the creepy loft and could hear voices downstairs, but they kept hushing each other up, and made creeper by the rocking horse that slowly rocks then stops and they gulp, calling out "please be good and stop you're freaking us out." Carl sneaked away when Mary saw from the corner of her eyes asked what he was doing, and he told her that he was checking on the kids.

The trunk wouldn't open until the footsteps could be heard coming into the loft when the kids hurdled together; at first, they screamed, then realized it was only Carl, their dad, and that's when the rocking chair rocked, and he screamed, and they laughed. They took his hand and told him it does that and not to worry; he wondered why they were so brave. He assisted them in gently opening the trunk, which proved to be a bit awkward at first, but it eventually yielded. To their surprise, the name on the trunk was Jeff, not Wendy's. Its initial contents didn't appear significant, but upon closer examination, they discovered that it was nearly empty, except for some concealed compartments.

What they uncovered was rather intriguing. Among the items hidden within were documents that provided evidence that Wendy was not a fraud, but rather, Jeff acted as the ringleader of an organization. This organization's aimed to deceive wealthy individuals by posing as clairvoyants and scamming them. Jeff had been involved in these activities, not out of choice but because the trunk was filled with his debts.

That's when Cheryl intervened and said to shock them, making them scream downstairs to the others. Dan asked what was wrong. Cheryl told them why the chair was moving; apparently, it was the last occupant trying to tell the kids that something was wrong. She, in fact, saw the souls and told Dan she was going to wake from her slumber.

That's when Sally, Jenny, Lily and Tom turned up wanting to see their mother, and Wendy had to dash to the phone to get her here at once and to explain when she got there that the energy never dies.

Its transferred back and forth until the energy escapes and landed into people. On that note, Wendy decided to complete her clairvoyant night, but Dan said as soon as this is over, I'm off to see Cheryl unless people want a lift back early. Not only that, they had to re-unite everyone properly.

Lucy and Edna arrived at the reunion apprehensive, their eyes darting around the room until they finally spotted Mia and Zane. "Thank goodness you're here," Zane said.

"Let's face the music together, but I have something to tell you when we have a minute. I think there is something off about this reunion; we have been looking people up.

It's not everyone from our year; something is amiss." They wandered to the registration table and found some people's names they knew, but Zane was right. The list did show other names. They thought it was a school reunion, but either way, they went to get a round of drinks and looked for, yes, two of the school bullies who slandered over and apologized for making their lives a misery; they are all grown up now, they said. Still, they all were very nervous and hesitant to accept; what were they really up to? They all excused themselves. Something was still wrong; they couldn't put their finger on it, so they went into the furthest corner to chat for now. Mia and Zane had the computer; Zane said, "I'm going stage. There's something up with Mia in toe. We will return soon".

Sometime later, Wendy was under duress from Jeff; she had a quick break and a quick word. She told him she couldn't pretend anymore; it was no good for her health. As the children came crashing into the room, they had overheard the conversation, told about what they heard, and were asked to leave. Everyone was all eyes on them, and then they suddenly went quiet, realizing the policeman was there and Jeff making a run through the designer trees. Wendy said something about two people who had been bullying her and were far away but at a reunion. But she couldn't see beyond that. Someone was telling her, but she didn't know anything else. That's when Dan had said as he was dashing to leave early that Edna and Lucy, his favorite visitors on the coach, had said something about the reunion. Still, they had gone even earlier than he had arranged to take them, but they needed to go, and Lucy seemed on edge, like she didn't want somebody to know her secret. But he pinpoint what was wrong Wendy and the others couldn't leave as they were all being questioned by the police, but Dan promised to give a statement first; he had to get back out of Blackpool with whoever was going and now to see if Cheryl had woken up. Outside, Jeff led a chase but ended up in handcuffs. He was informed of his rights and then led to the police station. Fortunately, because he knew the gardens well, he had managed to stir the police in the wrong direction initially, which gave him time to make a phone call, but to whom.

Chapter Five

Beep, Beep, Beep went the little monitor. Her eyes started to move, and her eyes were all a glaze; the nurse on duty was talking to her, but it sounded as if they weren't hers and the doctor was speaking in tongues, but it wasn't the nurse she could hear muffled voices, she was waking from her coma, but a slow process of acknowledging where she was, and was it real was she in the hospital? Trying to take the tubes out, which had to be taken out by the nurses. Her mouth was so dry she could hardly speak. They told her that she was clinically dead for a few minutes after the car accident, but as she was waking up slowly, she still could hear her voice.

She asked lots of questions once she had the chance, but from the corner of her eye, as the nurse was out of the room, she spotted a camera or what looked like one; she was left alone with her thoughts, trying desperately to get Dan, but she couldn't understand what was happening fully when the nurse comes in she voiced her concerns, she said quietly

"don't worry all will be revealed soon? as if she didn't want others to hear, but the funny thing is even though the nurse was keeping an eye on her, she still heard muffled voices, but couldn't see anything or anyone other than the doctors and nurse doing their job, there was a lot of activity in the corridors, but she was still very tired hopefully someone can help her recover.

Back at the reunion, although now in full swing, Mia finds a startling moment when she suddenly hides behind a pillar, hoping not to be seen because she comes across a camera crew. Her eyes widened, and she just about saw a split-screen banner and everything else apart from where they were sitting, not visible from the cameras. She just about managed to see with a stretch of the neck. The other screen was of a hospital, and she didn't know what she was seeing. She was about to tell Zane, but he ended up in a heated argument with a cameraman asking what was going on.

She got stopped by security along with Zane, and they were threatened to be led off the premises if they didn't be-have; they were taken to a room with monitors. They weren't sure the whole reunion was good; they had to tell the others, but the so-called bully was one of the cameramen.

They were producing a prank show about the afterlife, people's life's reactions and everyone except Dan had been filmed, as he was innocent and Cheryl was just unfortunate that she had a crash.

The only other family that wasn't filmed was Mary and her children, they had in fact been to Wendy's, on their own terms by car, but not involved except Wendy wasn't their real Aunt but she was by the missing paperwork found by the girls she was in fact a missing relative, who thought she was an Aunt and got revealed after the kids showed Wendy the slit in the draw to a separate compartment and in the loft was also amongst the papers proof of this, they still keep in touch though.

Back at the hospital, Cheryl, after some physio, had managed to drag herself to the shower, and there she was staring at a mirror and above that was a camera tucked near it; she screamed the place down, and then she had to be taken to bed and then got told by the hotshot producer, the was, in fact, the producer of a show afterlife and people's reactions to different scenarios apparently been working on a new script with her in it, she screamed again until the doctor came, but then she found out who the big producer was but was in fact related to Lucy, he found her reactions. Cheryl passed out from the news.

The hospital thought it was just a documentary, not realizing the full extent of the situation. They had fake letters too; they told the television company, or so they thought, they couldn't be there all day as Cheryl had to rest.

He then went to the reunion, only half an hour away. He finally found Lucy; he was, in fact, the producer, her husband. In fact, it was fake. She had just sat down after returning with two drinks at the reunion and told her it's been a prank, she nearly died, in fact, she passed out. He, in fact, was a bully and never changed at all. There were questions from Edna, "she buried you now." "She buried what she thought was me; I told her I was attending the conference.

She thought I had a heart attack. She had quickly arranged for burial before the weekend the ashes weren't mine; he then said, "Do you really think you can get ashes that quick, stupid woman? She believed everything I said. "At first, I felt sorry for her, and she was a good woman," but then he stopped as soon as Edna's eyes bore into him,

"but it was just ashes, nothing more; I wanted to see her reaction here and believe me she can go her own way after this I don't want her anymore," but Lucy sat there shivering not believing her eyes, and feel her eyes prickle she had to cry she had to. The big reveal cameras went up, and the story showed here and on the hospital television in Cheryl's room. Edna shouted at him, "You, you never change. Why did you even Marry her?" "I started to feel a little bit for her, just not enough. Then we had kids." "just leave us alone,"

Zane and Mia were let go and ran toward Edna and Lucy.

They had seen the whole thing on the screens in the back room, which meant the last few years, they had been followed. "and now it's time to sue," said Zane. The pressure was on, and they had to learn more about the show. Could they get paid as their lives had been filmed without their knowledge? Calling it a prank, they could do it, but Zane said again, "We will sue if you don't pay us and that poor woman in the coma; we have seen her on the other screen.

Where is she? I'm going to see her right now they reluctantly told him, as they had no choice but to give them the location he and Mia access they needed.

Whilst Lucy and Edna recovered from the shock, Lucy was even put in the recovery position whilst she came through, realizing the last year had been all lies Not only that, but Cheryl had lied to her x husband, and the policeman was corrupt too; once she gets out of there, she is going to ex-pose them all; in fact, when she comes too, she speaks into the camera and says: "once I'm out of here, I'm going to get you, you will see." Dan excused himself. They wouldn't let him leave initially, but he said, "You cannot stop me; I'm not part of this show. The policeman was about to arrest him when Wendy came to the hospital with backup, and the crooked policeman stopped. Jeff finally did the right thing. He can now have a lesser sentence, as they agreed.

Her ex-husband had already bolted from the scene and ran and was nowhere to be seen.

The afterlife indeed, but Cheryl now knows what happened the day of the crash as follows, Dan her most trusted friend and boyfriend was by her side in the hospital, and the whole story of how she ended up in the coma was the real story,

She was driving at High acres' rock and with its tight corners and twist it's a secluded place she was with Dan at the time, she was finding a nice place just him and her but it turns out that in front of her she had seen girls disappear into space through some sort of watch she had told Dan and as she turned to look again, he had tried to stop the car from crashing, but she had been driving too fast trying to get away from her x husband and crooked policeman, Dan was trying to slow her down but they got as far as Parkville, when he had noticed she had banged her head her unconscious but in fact it was the power from the crash, but it turns out someone was after her, her x husband and policeman when Dan had got out of the car he wanted the paper work she had uncovered, earlier that day when she had gone to his office.

Dan felt guilty as he was unscathed and he too had witnessed the girls in front disappear, people had disappeared up there without explanation before, and Cheryl's x husband and policeman left the seen in a hurry a soon as they saw she was unconscious and never to be seen until the hospital, not fully aware of the camera show until they realized they was in it, they had to keep a low profile but the policeman was in on everything and X husband made his escape after the hospital incident today but is on the run, whilst her husband has finally been arrested today, she knew too much and he couldn't save her. She was told a bad man had knocked her on the head, but in fact, it had been Dan by accident, as he had tried to stop the vehicle, so it was not technically his fault, and now it was time to confess, would she forgive him he did not know, but he loved her, and she loved him so time will tell.

She knew that the man's husband owed money to the policeman and involved him with Jeff, but also there was an incident about money laundering. The policeman actually knew these people had debts and had to get money. He had used people under the radar, and he could track them by being a policeman; they owed money, and Cheryl had seen the transactions, but by accident, when she went into his office, this story was not true. She had told half stories earlier; she had seen something suspicious about money, which looked like money laundering, but she couldn't prove it. Not only that, but he had only nipped out of the office for some lunch. She wanted some documents signed, so she made herself comfy when she accidentally came across the paperwork. She was always curious about what he did. Because Dan didn't want her to end up in some psych ward for saying she had seen people disappear before her eyes. She had also discussed the afterlife before the crash, and now they were filming her.

Chapter Six

THE AFTERLIFE INDEED WELL, Mrs. Bing (Jen), Mrs. Binglow (Mel) Sally, Jenny, Tom and Lily were firstly surprised that they were all related, the one big thing was that Wendy had managed to tell them after the kafuffle was she had news big news and wanted them to hold another session.

She was exhausted after today, but please stop over first thing in the morning. So as day grew into night, they started to wonder what she had to say, and she wouldn't say anything but "Just enjoy tonight."

They couldn't rest easy as they had been getting to know each other again, and that Deja vu situation kept coming up; the house was creaking a bit, and the sound of people creeping about but not there but then they kept hearing voices as if people were talking to each and every one of them until Wendy came down and said "don't worry I can see you're all restless Mel and Jen had already gone to sleep, the rest was about to go until this, but they said, "we want to go to bed, but we keep hearing, noises." "yes it's an old house"

said Wendy, Sally said "look things keep moving we cannot see the ghost, but we can hear them, again Wendy said I will tell you tomorrow I am too tired I'm off to bed help yourself to something to eat or drink, that will be it if you are still tired and hungry get some rest.

They ventured apprehensively to their assigned bedrooms; the girls were together, and Tom decided to sleep next door as the shadows came and went.

As adults, they still put their heads under the pillows.

They Read the big book with widened eyes they saw the picture of them, the watch and the family that disappeared through time, it's been too long, now their wish at the High Acres watch was to have normal lives in return they must do good, they do, but near High Acres there was other ghosts and instead of letting them share the magic of the watches, you used them for yourselves and the ghosts here have to forgive you, but although they do you as a family cannot accept,"

"accept what "you're dead."

They survived unscathed, but although they gathered for breakfast, they talked about their endeavors. Although slightly frightened, they were not frightened enough to leave after breakfast. Wendy had gathered everyone together, and one by one, they saw a giant book on the table; she told them she could do a reading on them but explained they were trapped within a loop and explained her friend would be here in ten minutes as the clock was big on the wall went slow at one time it seemed to go backwards, waiting for the ten minutes before her friend could arrive which ended up thirty minutes she had got delayed by traffic. Everyone was on the edge of their seats, waiting and waiting by this time.

They couldn't wait any longer. They cried out, "Please tell us." There was a lot of muffled chat between Wendy and her friend. They all held hands." And we have big news".

"Please tell us, we cannot stand this." "Well, you're in a loop. You end up here every year, and you cannot go home you will, but you need to realize the one thing: they were about to get up from the table but got told to sit.

Please listen to the story first.

"This happens each year you live normal lives, as you all requested many years ago. You keep trying to change history but end with Déjà vu.